The Ghosts
Of
Centre Street

A Haunting In Kingston

By

Michelle Dorey

MICHELLE DOREY

ॐॐॐॐ

DEDICATION

To my sister Corliss—
We made it across the ice!

MICHELLE DOREY

<u>Contents</u>

<u>Chapter One</u>

Barry Ryan's gaze shifted from the cell phone to the cab's window, spying the entrance to the doctor's office. Stella was one of his regulars; his was the only taxi she'd take to her various appointments for the last three years. But the pace of the appointments had picked up in the last month. What used to be every few weeks was now every other day. Well, at eighty-six, what would you expect?

He looked back down at his cell phone sitting in his lap, willing it to ring. Why hadn't Myra called? She said she'd do the test as soon as she got out of bed. His leg twitched a steady rhythm up and down under the steering wheel and he shifted once more in the seat. They'd been through pregnancy tests before, getting their hopes up, only to have them dashed a month later. But this time...this time was different, and he knew it. Myra would carry their daughter to term.

Yeah, and it was definitely a girl. Absolutely, unequivocally, a girl. He smiled picturing the baby in his arms. Even though his 'touch' told him what was going on, he still needed to hear it from the horse's mouth. He snorted. *Better not let Myra know about that metaphor!* They had been waiting and hoping and planning just for this for so long. Hell, they'd been married for years and Myra was getting nervous. Two more years for her and the big three-'O' would arrive.

The apartment would have to go. It was fine for just them, but with a kid? Way too cramped. Besides the neighbourhood was a little on the rough side—no place to raise a daughter.

He jumped at the buzzing cell phone. His mouth was suddenly dry. "Hi." It came out as a hoarse croak.

"Hey! It's positive! We're going to have a baby!" Myra's voice was full with delight. He could picture her wide green eyes, and the edge of her teeth biting her lower lip the way she always did when she was excited.

"Oh my God! I knew it! And you did the test correctly, the way—"

"I followed the directions exactly! It's true! I think the baby's due in June." She let out a squeal followed by bubbling laughter.

"June huh? Wow!" His hand gripped the phone tightly. June. That wasn't all that far away...only seven months. They would each really have to put in extra hours now so they could get a new place before she delivered.

Movement to the side caught his eye. The door of the doctor's office had opened. Stella had stepped out and her back was to him when she turned to say goodbye to the receptionist.

He did an eye roll and smiled. *Myra couldn't have called five minutes earlier?* "Sorry, babe, I gotta go; my passenger's here. I'll call you later. Love you!"

He clicked the phone off and opened the car door, hurrying up the set of stairs. It had rained earlier and with the carpet of wet leaves coating the sidewalk, it was more treacherous than usual for the old woman.

"Hold on!" He took the last two steps in one bound, placing his hand under her elbow. When the frail bones in her arm pressed his palm, she felt like a bird under the long dark coat.

"Holy doodle, it's a cold one today! Thanks, Barry, but I should be able to manage." Her steely blue eyes were framed by wrinkled, parchment skin. Thin, boney fingers curled around the iron railing like a claw.

"No way, Stella. With the wind today, you'd blow away like a leaf." He tightened his grip as she gingerly descended the first step. "What'd the doctor say? You gonna live?"

Her eyes closed for a moment. "Hmph!" Opening them, she gestured at the car. "Let's skedaddle." She resumed maneuvering the granite steps silently.

Barry's gut tightened and he looked at her closely. Normally, there was a friendly banter back and forth between them when he asked her this. She'd always counter with a line about outliving the fool doctor, but not today. That wasn't good.

He opened the front door of the cab and held her arm when she turned to take a seat. Her legs above the clunky, orthotic shoes were like twigs, the tan support stockings wrinkled at her ankles. She'd really aged in the last month.

Forcing a smile, he shut the door and strode once more to the driver's side. When he got in, her head was turned away, gazing out the side window.

He took a deep breath. It was worth one more try to cheer her up. "Where to now? Not the Royal Tap Room again? Y'know, you can't spend every afternoon there, flirting with all the young stud muffins." He reached to tap her knee and grinned when she turned to face him. "I'm your driver, not your body guard."

Again, his gut sank to the floor when the familiar joke only resulted in a wan smile. He sighed and this time his voice was serious. "Stella? You're not really okay, are you?"

10

Her eyes focused on his and she watched him silently for a few moments. "How is Myra doing? I'm sure you know it's a little girl she's carrying, right?"

The look of surprise on his face must have been the reason that *finally*, her lips twitched in a grin. She'd known? Hell, only he and Myra knew she was pregnant and *that* was just confirmed ten minutes ago!

"Everything will work out well. Don't worry, Barry. The money and the house will be there when your daughter arrives. And June...it's the best month of the year." Her eyes filmed over with tears and she took a deep breath, shaking her head to dispel the sudden sadness.

"How the hell—?"

She let out a whisper of a laugh. "You think you're the only person in the world with... what do you call it? The *touch*?" She let out another 'Hmpf' and again laughed lightly. "Me? I've always called it the *grace*." She patted his knee. "I *know* things, Barry. Just like you, I can see the future and sense...well, let's just say, I sense things, too."

Slowly, his eyes closed for a moment. This meant a lot to her, talking about this. And...she had desperate health issues that couldn't be ignored any longer. Fear and sorrow emanated from her tiny body, cloaking her in a dark cloud. How much time did she have left before...?

11

As he worked the car through traffic, he kept glancing over at her. She was watching him closely.

Holy doodle, the irony's so rich! He jumped in his seat. Stella's voice was in his head?

She gave a sharp laugh. "Oh dear, the look on your face, Barry!" She stared at him again.

Just like birds of a feather, Barry, we don't really need words.

He yanked the car to the curb, stopping at a fire hydrant.

"How are you doing that!" He wasn't scared, but shit, that was a surprise!

Watch your language, young man. Why can't you say 'doodle' instead?

"Stella…" he croaked, this is a lot to absorb."

"Okay, okay… I understand." She sighed. "I guess I should have come clean with you earlier." She looked away. "But like all people, I thought I had all the time in the world." She chuckled. "What a silly old woman." She turned back to him. "As I was saying, the irony is compelling." She laid her hands primly on her lap and looked back at him.

"What's that supposed to mean, anyway?"

Slowly shaking her head, she replied, "Well, you *knew* that Myra was pregnant before she phoned you, but even so, you needed to hear it…" she wiggled her eyebrows at him, "straight from the horse's mouth." She let out another bark of laughter at the look on Barry's face.

"You…"

"Yes, you ninny. But that's not my point. My point is that I know my time's very short, but it really didn't… I don't know… it didn't *count* maybe, until that fool doctor told me just now." She looked over at the fire hydrant and gestured with a hand. "Let's get me home, alright?"

"Okay." He put the car in gear and wheeled back into traffic.

Shit! He sighed. There was nothing he could do to change the fact of her death. She was old and her time was close. Any fool could see that; you didn't need to be psychic to know it.

He felt Stella's hand on his arm, like a sparrow landing. "You've been like a son to me these past couple of years—making sure I get to the doctor, carting my groceries, and even shoveling my walkway the last three winters. You've been kind to me, Barry."

"You're easy to be kind to, toots." His eyes were starting to sting.

"Bull patootie. How many other people do you bring presents to, when it's their birthday? But more than that, you treat me like an equal, not some foolish old woman." Her hand was now patting his arm, and he took a deep breath.

It's not REALLY goodbye.

"Barry."

He glanced over at her and her face was solemn.

"Barry, I never told you the date I was born." She jabbed a finger at him. "*I never told you my birthday.*" She dropped her hand back to her lap. "You have the second sight, son...same as me. It's time you accepted that about yourself." She sighed and shook her head. "Quick. Think of a number."

He tried to sidestep her suggestion, but eleven sixty three popped into his head, part of the title of a book he was reading.

Immediately, she spoke again. "Eleven sixty three. Now guess my number."

No! But like before, the words flashed before his eyes. He sighed. "Ninety-nine."

"See?" She clucked her tongue and this time when she reached for his hand she gave it a quick squeeze. Her voice hitched when she spoke. "I just wish I had more time... I would have liked to be able to hold your daughter."

"You'll probably outlive me, Stella. As far as my daughter and holding her—"

"STOP IT! I've wanted to have this conversation with you for a long time. I always knew you didn't want to go down this road but there isn't much time left. Having the grace, the touch...the sixth sense is part of who you are, Barry. Accept it. It's important." Her blue eyes pierced through to his soul.

He snorted, once more trying to make light of it and dodge this conversation. "Not to me it isn't. Being happy, not hurting other people, that's what's important."

"What happened to your mother wasn't your fault, Barry." Her voice was soft and she reached over to squeeze his hand. "You saw something and you told her. We see only one of many outcomes which can happen. Your mother's free will, her *choice* made the difference."

A picture of his mother flashed in his mind and he shook his head, erasing the image like the etch-o-sketch he'd played with as a kid. Stella 'knew' too much. He couldn't fool her but he didn't need to talk about it either. It was still too painful to deal with. He had put it out of his mind and that's where it would stay, by hell!

"Barry? All I'm saying is, don't fight it any more. It's a gift, kind of like being a child prodigy...being able to play classical music on the piano when you're only four. Be aware of it, and don't be afraid to use your gift. You going to need to at some point." Stella sat back and closed her eyes.

Some gift! If anything it was a curse that brought more complications to his life than solutions. Not to mention the beat downs he'd gotten as a kid in school for 'being weird'. And the one time he *should* have used it, he didn't... He could have saved his mother, but kept his mouth shut.

He sighed. Still...he liked Stella. He looked over at her and his throat clenched, fighting tears that burned behind his eyes. There wasn't much time. She was going to die soon. The exact time was vague in his mind. It could be a week or even tomorrow.

He reached over and touched her shoulder. "Stella, do you have any relatives left? Do you need me to call anyone...when... well, you know...?"

Her eyes opened and she shook her head, and closed them again.

He felt her presence leave just as he turned the car down the laneway leading to her stately Victorian era home; all of her essence that remained was a hint lilac in the air. A booming burst of thunder made him jump and he watched as raindrops the size of marbles railed down on the windshield. With a sigh he reached over to Stella and shook her arm.

"Stella? We're here."

A lonesome sadness engulfed him as he stared at her for a moment. She wasn't moving at all.

"Stella." His fingers tightened on her wrist, shaking her harder.

The only response was the bobbing of her head, eyes still closed while her lips had parted slightly. Barry sat still as a stone, watching her, his breath hitched tight in his chest. This couldn't be happening. He felt like a zombie staring out the windshield. Nothing seemed real.

The rain poured down in torrents and an occasional spark of lightening flashed across the now blue-black sky. The outline of the two storey, grey limestone house blurred and wavered in the sheets of water rippling on the glass. From where he sat in the circular driveway before the entrance the home was imposing. The same thought he had every time he drove up to it, once again entered his mind: '*What the hell is an old woman doing living in such a huge place*?' He looked back over to Stella's body. Well, not anymore.

Like dark eyes, the two windows bordering the gabled entrance peered down at him. When the lightening flared once more, there was a shadow of a figure in the top floor window that vanished along with the flash of light.

Barry's head jerked forward sucking in a gulp of air, staring at the image. But as quickly as it had

17

appeared, it vanished, and only darkness showed in the glass. The hair on the back of his neck tingled and his shoulders rolled in a soft shudder. He could have sworn that there'd been a woman in the window and she'd waved at him, but Stella lived alone.

When he turned to the old lady once more, curiosity mingled with the grief in his gaze. For all the times he'd ferried her around, he really didn't know much about her life. Who really, was Stella Braithwaite?

<u>Chapter Two</u>

He was just finishing dressing when Myra stirred awake. Damn it. He should have grabbed his clothes and put them on in the bathroom.

She sat up in bed. "You're sure you don't want me to come?"

Barry gave his head a small shake. "No, you stay home. It's going to be…" he shrugged. "Sad." He looked away. "Forlorn, actually. There won't be any mourners besides me, and she was a nice woman…" He sighed.

"You said her lawyer's going to be there though, right?"

He nodded. "Yeah. There's a will and one of its mandates is, it's to be read on the day of her funeral." He gave a small smile. "I guess I'm getting some sort of bequeath from her." He stepped to the closet and grabbed his blue blazer and put it on. "How do I look?"

19

Myra smiled. "It shrunk a bit. Not too much, but it could use some taking out."

He gave a small wave and grin. "That's the cigarettes. Two years off the butts and I really didn't put that much weight on." He brushed off his sleeve. "Pretty fly if you ask me. And considering that I spend my entire workday on my ass behind the wheel of a cab, pretty good."

Myra laughed. "Yeah. Right. Me kicking you out of the apartment every night to go for a half hour walk has *nothing* to do with it!" She lay back on the bed and pointed to her belly. "Time for the checkup."

"No problem." He stepped over to the bed and laid his hand on her stomach. He smiled. "She says 'Yo, mama'"

Myra's eyes flew open wide. "Really? She knows we're here? Ohmygod!"

He burst out laughing. "No! I'm just kidding! She's asleep. She's pretty much always asleep. And even when she's awake, it's like she's dozing."

Myra thumped him in the shoulder. "Funny guy. You really got me." She sat back up. "I'm glad that you're using your touch again, Barry. It makes me feel good to know that you can sense her."

He never told her that he had sensed the previous two pregnancies that had ended in miscarriage.

As soon as he felt Myra quicken, he knew those poor things were doomed. Instead, he nodded back to her. "Yeah, well...this one's a keeper, and I don't mind getting to know her early on."

Myra rubbed her stomach. "Early on? That's an understatement." She cocked her head at him. "You know it's funny. It's the first time since you told me about the touch that you've ever let me see you use it."

"I know." He sat on the bed and slipped his shoes on.

"Think you'll use it more?" She bobbed her eyebrows at him. "You know, we can go to the casino and make a killing at roulette or something."

He laughed. "That has *never* worked for me!" He spread out his arms. "If it did, you think we'd be living in this dump?" Since they found out about Myra being pregnant, two days ago, their cozy 'love nest' of a one bedroom apartment had become almost claustrophobic to him. They barely had enough money salted away to move into a nice two bedroom in one of the newer high rises, and with Myra being two months along he was going to have to drive extra shifts and stretch out his other days. She wasn't going to get much of a maternity leave from her waitress job.

Myra nodded. "Yeah, I know; but still a gal's gotta hope, right?"

He patted her leg. "We'll be okay. It's a pretty good life so far, isn't it?" The last eight years had been the happiest of his life, ever since their first date.

She made a face and shrugged. "Doesn't suck."

He barked a laugh and stood up. "And with that glowing testament, I shall take your leave!"

Closing the apartment door and shrugging into his overcoat, the smell of cigarettes wafted in the air of the narrow hall and stairwell. The muscle in his jaw tightened. They really needed to move to a new place soon. The cigarette smell was so wrong. Sure he quit smoking, but there wasn't a day that went by that he didn't miss the old treacherous friend. He certainly didn't want his daughter exposed to it.

Outside, the day was typical November, grey and bleak, threatening rain—perfect for a funeral. He got into his taxi and started the engine. Stella. He sighed and drove out from the parking lot onto the street and headed towards Reid's Funeral Home over on Johnson Street.

****

The funeral, if that's what one could call it, was as sad and forlorn as the cold autumn day. There was just himself and Stella's lawyer, an older Asian man-- Jack Chang. Barry knew the guy; he was fairly active in issues around the city, popping up at fund raisers for the

United Way, Big Brothers and Sisters and other charities. His office was over on King Street in the older, gentrified part of the city.

The two men shook hands in the viewing room before Stella's casket and made their introductions.

"Did you know Ms. Braithwaite very long?" the lawyer asked.

"About three years or so," Barry felt a little embarrassed. "I'm her favorite cabby, but that's all."

"I see, I see," the guy said, nodding. "Are you sure? Three years?" He was a slight guy, and peered up at Barry through his eyeglasses, tilting his head in curiosity.

"Yeah, pretty sure. Maybe a little longer." Barry shrugged. "I've only been driving a cab for the last four years— ever since those guys closed the old DuPont plant, you know?"

"I see..." Jack looked puzzled.

"What's the big deal?" The expression on the lawyer's face had gone from curiosity to outright puzzlement as he stroked his chin.

"But no more than four years, correct?"

"That's right." Barry put his hands on his waist.

Chang looked down at his feet. "Very curious."

"Hey, Mr. Chang, what's wrong?"

"Nothing, I suppose." Chang shrugged. "I'll explain after the services. You know we need to return to my office after the interment, right?"

"Yeah, you told me that yesterday. Thanks for letting me know about the funeral." Barry held up a hand for a moment. "By the way, how did you get my cell phone number to get hold of me anyway?"

Chang tilted his chin at Stella's coffin. "Ms. Braithwaite stopped in my office the week before she passed away with the information."

"Oh. Okay."

At that point, the funeral director came into the visiting room. He introduced himself and told them that there would be no prayers, eulogy or any such ritual. Misters Chang and Ryan were the only mourners expected per Ms. Braithwaite's instruction, and when they arrived they were to immediately proceed to the cemetery.

"That's it?" said Barry. "Sounds kind of cold if you ask me."

"Those were her instructions, Sir," the mortician said, holding out his hands palm up. "At least we can respect her final wishes, right?"

"I guess." Barry stepped over to where the plain casket rested. He placed his hand on the burnished maple surface. "If that's what you want toots, it's fine by me," he said patting it. "Just for the record, I'm gonna miss you." His breath hitched. He really liked the old woman; more than he knew until she died. God damn it.

Watch your language young man!

His head jerked up and he looked around. There was just the lawyer and undertaker standing there. He turned back to the coffin and said in the lowest of whispers, "Holy shit."

Barry! A little respect for the dearly departed! Say doodle!

A tear formed in the corner of his eye when he heard the smile in that voice. "Holy doodle." He turned to the two men. "Okay, let's get this show on the road, okay?"

As they wheeled the casket to the waiting hearse, his heart was light.

****

At the gravesite, there were no prayers nor last words other than Chang saying 'May she rest in peace'. After the attendants lowered the casket into the ground, Barry took a handful of earth that was piled at the side of the grave and threw it in.

Bye, toots.

I'll see you around, big boy.

He snorted and he and Chang headed to their cars. They would meet at Jack's law office for the reading of the will.

****

When he got out of the car, he noticed a guy in a dark overcoat step over to Mr. Chang at the entrance, extending his hand. Barry's eyes narrowed watching the burly man talk *at* the old lawyer, his face flushed and angry, towering over the shorter man. It looked like Stella wasn't exactly telling the truth when she said she had no relatives.

As he walked up to the two men, he reached out with the touch. The weasel in the dark coat smelled money and was there to make sure he got his share. Barry's gut tightened watching him. He seemed familiar somehow but he was sure he'd never met him before. His eyes narrowed. There was something bad about that guy. The three men entered the office.

"It will take me a few minutes to prepare everything," Mr. Chang said. "Make yourselves comfortable, please." He stepped from the waiting room into his office.

****

Gordon Braithwaite filled the chair in the waiting room at John Chang's office. Barry, sitting across from him picked up a *Yachting* magazine and pretended to skim through it. Chang had introduced them at door and Gordon had barely acknowledged him, preferring to bend the lawyer's ear with his puffery and self righteousness. It was obvious from the way the guy fidgeted in his seat, emitting long loud sighs that he was impatient with the whole thing. Just give him the money and he'd be off in a shot.

The middle aged secretary sitting behind the high counter peered over her glasses and cleared her throat before speaking. "Mr. Chang will see you gentlemen now."

Before they were even on their feet, John Chang appeared in the crack of the door, giving a small nod of his head before disappearing inside.

Gordon brushed by Barry, knocking his shoulder in the process and not even bothering to say he was sorry or 'excuse me'. Barry's jaw muscle worked as he walked by the secretary, following the rude hulk into Chang's inner lair. If the occasion wasn't so solemn, he'd be tempted to jostle him right back or say something sarcastic but for now, he'd just let it go.

The guy was almost as tall as Barry's six foot four, but where Barry was downright skinny, this guy had spent a lot of time making friends with the Burger King. His grey hair was slicked back and his gut billowed over the belt of cheap slacks. Barry could smell the booze on the guy's breath and it wasn't even ten in the morning. He shook his head and followed the oaf into the private chambers.

He lowered into an empty chair, noting that Gordon was perched close to Chang's desk, straining forward to scan the sets of paper on the worn, wooden surface.

Barry's eyes met Mr. Chang's for a moment, before the lawyer cleared his throat to begin. "I knew Stella Braithwaite for a number of years. She was both a client and a friend. She drew up her last will and testament ten years ago and was here just last week to ensure everything was in order." Again he shot a look at Barry that was puzzled. His nimble tan fingers pushed the two sets of documents towards Barry and Gordon.

Barry reached for them and sat back, his eyes focused on the official document.

Beside him Gordon blurted, "Just give us the Coles notes version. What did she leave me?" He tapped the papers and shoved them back at the elderly lawyer.

For a moment the lawyer's mouth fell open and even in the leathered, dark face, the flush of red in his cheeks was obvious. His words were clipped when he spoke. "Very well, Mr. Braithwaite." He took a deep breath and the corners of his lips twitched. "Stella left the bulk of her estate to Mr. Ryan. You receive one dollar, ensuring that as a blood relative, your interests were considered in her decision."

Gordon burst out of his chair. "What the hell? She can't do that!" Braithwaite looked like he was about to explode, his face a peppery red and voice booming in the small office.

Barry paid little attention to the big lout beside him, the blood was roaring in his ears from what he'd just read on his copy of the will. He sat still, his hands shaking as he scanned the clauses and his eyes locked on the amount of money, written in bold font. *Two million dollars*!

Gordon was still blustering, arguing with the lawyer, threatening to lodge a complaint with the bar association, go to the Supreme Court, the press, anything, while Jack Chang countered each threat in a soft-spoken, rational voice.

It was a dull backdrop to the shock waves rippling through Barry's body.

He'd suspected she had a nest egg but this...this was *way* over the top. It was also the answer to their problems! They could afford a nice apartment. Hell! Even a *house* with that kind of money! Someplace nice with a back yard and mature trees for a swing and...

"Bloody shyster!" Gordon, now screaming, broke through Barry's daydream. "How much of a kick-back do you get from this clown here?"

Thud! The chair next to Barry, toppled onto the floor making Barry startle. Gordon towered high, bent over the desk like a gargoyle, the knuckles of his fists pressing against the dark wood.

Gordon turned to Barry, "As for you, ya goof, don't spend that money, yet!" Gordon stepped by him and continued the loud harangue from the doorway. "You're not dealing with just anybody here. I *know* people, lawyers and judges, *important people*. I've worked in the penitentiary for forty years! It's filled with con artists like you two. You won't get away with this!" He stepped out into the hallway and slammed the door so hard the window across the room shook.

Jack Chang sat there, his hands trembling. "I'm having a hard time being inscrutable, you know. What a prick!"

Barry stood and put the chair back in place. "No wonder Stella didn't leave him anything." He sat back down in his own chair.

"Stella warned me her nephew, Gordon Braithwaite, would try to make trouble." Jack Chang sighed. He leaned over the top of his desk. "Now, Mr. Ryan, she set a condition in order for you to make claim of the inheritance." He opened the black laptop computer on the side of his desk and peered down his nose eyeing the screen while his fingers tapped, booting the machine to life.

Barry's shoulders slumped and he pulled his chair closer to the desk, trying to keep the disappointment from showing on his face. Of course. The money had been too good to be true. There had to be strings attached.

The lawyer's sharp brown eyes flickered to Barry for a moment and he continued. "She had me videotape her as she explained the terms." He looked sharply at Barry in silence for a full thirty seconds. "I had to transfer the tape to my computer a while ago, but it is still valid. Ms. Braithwaite and I watched it together just last week."

Finally, he took a deep breath and turned the screen so that Barry could see it. As he clicked the icon, starting the recording, he mumbled softly. "A bit unusual, but entirely legal."

Stella's pale face, framed by her white hair filled the screen and for a moment she looked scared, her gaze darting past the focus of the camera to something behind the person filming. "Am I on? Is this thing working?"

"Could you pause for a second?" Barry asked. When Jack pressed the button, he leaned forward to the screen. Stella looked terrific! She must have gone to a salon or something before making the tape. She looked years younger than his last memory of her. He shook his head. "Women, huh?" He smiled at Jack.

"I suppose. May I continue?" When Barry nodded, he pressed the button again and the recording continued.

On the screen, at the soft assent of the lawyer, Stella sat straighter and managed a small smile. "Barry, if you're seeing this, then I won't be needing any cab rides to the quack anymore."

Barry's throat became tight and he swallowed hard, fighting a tear. He was trying to be strong—as strong and light-hearted as Stella recording this, had been. Her doctor's appointments on Tuesdays, the wisdom and humor in her blue eyes, her kindness...all gone now. Even the expression she always used—holy doodle—not holy cow or holy mackerel—was quirky. She was like an ancient, eccentric aunt who brought a spark of joy to his day.

"I am leaving my house and money to you, Barry. For over sixty years I have lived there. It's a beautiful home but it's also..." She sighed and looked away for a moment before continuing. "...also unique. I first came to live there when my aunt became ill. Aunt Evelyn had the 'second sight', and she wanted me to continue living in the house after she passed."

Her chin rose higher and a look of determination was in her piercing eyes. "It's imperative that a person with the 'sight' live there. I have left the cash in my estate... to be dispersed to you upon the completion of a year that you reside in the house."

She chuckled and once more her gaze drifted higher, looking past the camera. "Listen to me. Ha! I'm starting to sound like a lawyer, Jack. You're a bad influence."

The lawyer sitting behind his desk, dropped his gaze and his hand rubbed the back of his neck. There was a small smile on his face. He was probably remembering the recording session with Stella. She'd been such a tease.

"In plain language, live there for a year and the money's yours, Barry. I'm confident that you and your family will be happy there. You won't want to leave, just like I never did. The house sits on very powerful land." She chuckled. "Some would say hallowed ground but I was never much into that kind of thing."

Barry glanced over at the lawyer to see if he showed any sign of understanding. 'hallowed ground'? The lawyer shrugged and shook his head.

Stella's voice continued and Barry turned back to the screen.

"I can picture the bewildered look on your face and wish I were there right now to give you a poke in

33

the ribs. Just trust me for now on this. As you live in the house over time, things will become clearer. You'll see."

She leaned closer to the camera and her eyes were intense. "The house needs you as much as you need the house." Her smile was like the burst of sunshine behind a bank of clouds. "Remember, my body may be dead, but energy cannot be destroyed. It just changes." With a final smile, she said in the Mae West voice she had used so often in his cab; her last words were "See you around, big boy."

The recording ended and Barry wiped his eyes and looked up to see Mr. Chang again watching him closely.

"What! What's your problem! I never did nor said a single thing for her to do that!" he said. "Why are you looking at me like that?"

Jack tapped the surface of his desk, his chin resting in his hand. "You met her for the first time just four years ago."

"Yeah, that's right."

"When you were a boy, did you mow her lawn or deliver her newspapers?"

"What? No! I didn't grow up in that part of the city!"

Jack shook his head. "Very curious."

"You said that back at the funeral home. What's your problem?"

Jack tapped the side of his computer. "I made the original recording with a video camera."

"So? I got one on my phone."

Jack shook his head slightly. "No, a video recording camera. A video tape. I had it transferred to digital last week at Ms. Braithwaite's request."

"Okay. You sort of said that before."

"A VHS tape, Mr. Ryan."

"I heard you the first time, Mr. Chang."

Chang shook his head again. "I'm not being clear because I'm so baffled." He put his hands on the desktop. "That recording you just saw? I made it more than twenty years ago."

Chapter Three

That same evening, Myra finished up her shift at the restaurant for the day. It had been a busy shift and she was beat to a snot. Two months along in her pregnancy and the baby was sucking energy from her like a vampire. She patted her stomach. Not that she was complaining, the tips had been good, and she had supper in hand. Nothing like an employee discount from working in a restaurant to take the edge off a hard day's work!

She had sent Barry a text telling him she was ready to go home, but didn't hear back. Oh man, she hoped he wasn't on some out of town call. She didn't want to have to wait for the bus; the day was dreary enough.

Cars whipped by on the street, busy with the usual crowd getting off work and hurrying home. She pulled her collar higher at the gust of icy air buffeting her face and turned to stride down the sidewalk to the bus stop.

"Hey Myra!"

Hearing Barry's voice, she spun around. There he was, leaned over the front seat of the cab, a big grin on his face, peering at her through the open, passenger side window.

Eight years married, and still he was great looking, even with that broken nose he got as a kid. He needed a haircut, his brown locks were pretty tousled. Those pale blue eyes of his shone from his fair complexion. She once described him as having a peaches and cream complexion, and he laughed at her for calling him 'girly'. He was stopped in the street blocking traffic and was waving at her to get in.

She grabbed the door handle and hopped in to escape the blustery day. After planting a big kiss on his cheek she tugged the seat belt over her.

"How'd it go today? Anyone else at the funeral?" She turned to look at him, trying to read the expression on his face. The old lady's death had really bothered him. Much more so than she would have expected, considering she was just a customer, even if one of his regular ones.

"Just me and the lawyer. Her only relative, her nephew showed up at Jack Chang's office afterwards."

Barry shook his head. "What a total jerk." He snorted and the car started moving again.

"Poor Stella. That's kind of sad." Myra wiggled her toes in her work shoes. She hadn't sat down for more than five minutes all day with the steady stream of customers. The rain and chilly weather helped keep the restaurant business hopping. Even though she had a great set of footwear for work—as good as any nurse's shoes, her feet hurt like hell. They were starting to swell a little, which was pretty early in her pregnancy. Thank God she grabbed dinner to-go. She couldn't wait to get home and take a hot bath.

When Barry changed lanes and flipped the turn signal on, she frowned. "Where're you going? This is the opposite direction to home."

"I want to show you something." Barry looked over at her his eyes showing excitement, even though he kept his voice matter of fact. He turned back to the road, rubbing his hand up and down the leg of his pants. Under his crooked but cute nose, the corner of his mouth twitched.

She had to smile despite feeling so weary. He was like a kid giving his Dad a gift at Christmas, trying to keep a happy secret, but busting to tell it. "Something good, I take it?" She inhaled deeply, feeling a rush of love for her crazy guy.

"It depends." He turned and the sudden seriousness in his eyes was a little unsettling.

She decided to play it lightly even though a pall had dampened her spirit. "Depends on whether we can afford it? Depends on my mood, whether you'll get lucky tonight or—"

"Shush! You'll never guess, so don't even try." He reached over and squeezed her knee, running his hand higher up her leg in the tan stockings. "How was work? Make me some money, honey?"

"Yeah, it was a pretty good day, over a hundred and fifty bucks. Joanne called in sick so I was crazy busy." Her head bobbed forward when a thought from that morning hit her. "What'd you see the lawyer about? Don't tell me that old lady left you something."

He pressed the accelerator harder when the light turned orange, getting through the intersection quickly. There was a smile on his face when he glanced over at her. "Stella. Her name was Stella." He took a breath. "I'll never forget her."

She grinned and closed her eyes for a moment. It was actually one of the endearing things about Barry— the kindness and respect he showed to other people. Even though he'd gently put her in her place, she loved him like crazy. "Okay. Sorry. Stella." She held her hands out palms up. "So, you get us some money, honey?"

When he flipped the turn signal once more, waiting for traffic to clear, she frowned. "Barry?"

"Patience, young Jedi," he said. He was maneuvering the car up West Street. He went through the Queen's University campus and continued down Union Street, past the homes that doubled as student rentals and into a more genteel and older part of the city. Many of these homes had been built as single family dwellings over a century ago. She looked out the window with a twinge of envy as they passed houses with circular driveways and detached garages. She didn't like to think about it, but the garages were twice the size of the apartment they lived in.

"Barry," she said, holding up the plastic bag with their takeout supper. "Dinner will get cold, and it's your fave— chicken marsala with 'shrooms."

He glanced over. "We'll eat soon, don't worry." He gave her a cheese grin. "That is, if you'll be able to eat!" He turned the car down Center Street. Lake Ontario was just a block or two away.

"You want to eat outside by the lake? In this weather? Barry, do you have a screw loose or something?"

He ignored her and turned into a circular driveway, stopping in front of a two storey limestone house. When he turned to her, there was a mile-wide grin on his face. "Honey, we're home!"

40

Chapter Four

She stood in front of the huge building, her head tilted back. Before her was a set of five steps that ascended to an expansive portico that had a balcony railing on top. She knew that balcony would lead to the master bedroom. Their bedroom.

The massive limestone walls continued past to a pointed arch which spread out to a hip roof covering the rest of the home she supposed. At the top of the roof, not one, but two wide chimneys reached further up to the grey sky.

Her gaze went to the left and right of the building, seeing the walkways that went around to the back yard.

Barry's warm hand took hers and they silently climbed the stairs to the entrance. He took a set of keys from his pocket and opened the door. It was a thick, heavy door, and in the center was a cut glass window.

Still wordlessly, they stepped into the foyer.

41

She wrapped her arms around herself, gazing numbly around. The right of the foyer was taken up by a cherry wood entryway bench that was longer than their living room sofa. On the left, a boot rack, hall tree and umbrella stand were placed. The foyer was bigger than their bedroom.

Myra turned to her husband to see him smiling down at her. She turned back and stepped into the main hallway. Enormous rooms to her left and right, each one larger than their own apartment bracketed a wide central staircase that would lead up to even grander and more spacious rooms she had ever stepped foot in.

She turned to Barry again.

"She gave this to you?"

He nodded with a smile. "To us, hon. That whole marriage thing, y'know?"

"No more Montreal Street?" She saw him nod his head. No more hookers walking the stroll on Friday and Saturday nights? No more listening to foul mouthed fights in their building on the weekends after the Social Services checks came in? No more hallways stinking of cigarette smoke?

Barry nodded as if he'd heard her thoughts. "That's right. None of it."

She reached out to him with one hand, the other holding her womb.

And burst into tears.

****

Barry held his weeping wife and his own shoulders quaked as well. As she emptied out the shock and surprise he looked around the house. He had never been past the foyer. Glancing over, to the coat rack and bench he saw Stella's heavier coat and boots already placed neatly in anticipation of the coming winter. His chest tightened. He would never see her in those things again.

It took Myra just a minute to collect herself. She took a deep breath tilted her head up at him. Stepping away, she tugged him by the hand. "Let's check this place out!"

Her tears gone, her face was now a huge grin over her Betty Boop blue eyes. Stepping into the hallway, Barry took a sniff of the air. There was an ancient smell of lemon wax and old books, kind of a library smell. It wasn't unpleasant, just kind of different than he would have thought. He gave his head a small shake. Hell! What had he expected? What was a 'house of power' supposed to smell like?

When he stepped on the wooden floorboard, it groaned in protest, as if in mourning for Stella's lighter footstep.

Myra let go of his hand and skipped into the dining room. When he followed her through a wide archway, she stood staring at the huge dining room table, piled high with books and papers.

She picked up a book and looked over at him. "Stella liked to read, didn't she?"

"It explains how she was always up on current events. She was sharp as a tack."

Myra set the book down and looked around the room from the antique sideboard up to the ceiling. "Wow! These ceilings must be ten feet tall!"

Barry stretched his hand over his head, eyeing the distance between it and the ceiling. "Twelve! I'm six feet and my hand doesn't come close to that height."

She stepped over to him and kissed his cheek. "We'll be able to have a real Christmas tree...a huge one!"

The excitement in her eyes was contagious! He'd been trying to control his emotions, look objectively at the house but it was getting harder and harder to do that. "Wonder what it would cost to heat this place?"

Myra rolled her eyes and started off to the next area of the house. "Who cares? I'll wear sweaters and long underwear! This place is gorgeous."

He put his hands in his pockets and looked around the room, at the high windows. The sill under it had to be over a foot deep, set in the thick limestone. The woodwork was original and in pretty good condition.

"Barry! Quick! Come see this!"

He grinned at the excitement in her voice. She was usually pretty upbeat, but like him, for the last while she'd been concerned about money and the new baby. It was great to hear her happiness. *Wait till I tell her about the money on top of this place!*

He strode through the archway and into a big, country kitchen, dominated by a large window. It overlooked the backyard, where there was a small garden and a stately maple tree extending its now bare limbs to the sky. At the very back of the lot was a willow tree and even from where he stood, Barry could see a glimmer of water from a small pond. He saw tall fences surround the property. This place was an oasis.

Myra had again taken off on her explorations. She went to the room on the opposite side of the hallway from the dining room and Barry followed. She stopped as soon as she crossed the threshold. Her shoulders convulsed in a small shudder. "Brrr...why's this room so cold?"

He'd felt it too, as soon as he entered. The temperature had to be at least ten degrees cooler than the other rooms. The hair on his arms and neck tingled and his gaze darted around for a moment or two. There was nothing that he could see, but the sense they weren't alone, was strong.

Myra's nose wrinkled. "I'm not crazy about this room."

They stepped out of the room and the downbeat evaporated. Going to the staircase, he folded her into his arms again. A thought popped into his mind. "I want to name the baby after Stella."

Her smile was coquettish when she stepped closer. "What if it's a boy? Maybe Stella was wrong about it being a girl."

"It's a girl. Trust me." He slid his hand over her body, resting it on her tummy.

Her nose wrinkled again. "But Stella? I'm not sure I like that name. How about Isabella? It' sounds a little like Stella, don't you think?"

'Yes. I like that.' It was a soft whisper in his head. The same Stella voice from the funeral. He'd had premonitions before, even answers to questions pop into his mind, but never actual vocalizations, words spoken in his head, until the last few days. And it had been Stella's voice.

There was just the faintest of touches on the back of his neck, making him roll his shoulders and pull

THE GHOSTS OF CENTRE STREET

his head higher. It was a definite affirmation of her presence. She'd said she'd be around. It was becoming clear she'd never left...well, not entirely. His gaze darted around the room, looking for further sign of the woman, but there was only tiny dust particles in the air, highlighted by the soft light from the window.

His eyes met Myra's. "Isabella it is. I like it." He stepped back and took her hand, leading the way. "Let's see the upstairs."

Chapter 5

They had gone through the house to find it neat as a pin and pretty much move in ready. In the bedrooms upstairs, each bed was stripped and dust covers were set over the furniture. The linen closet though, was filled with laundered sheets, pillowcases, facecloths and towels.

All of the pots and pans in the kitchen, as well as the dishes and cutlery were spic and span.

"She knew she was dying," said Barry, taking Myra's hand as they went back towards the front of the house. "She cleaned the place out as best as she could for us."

The amount of clutter was a minimum. The only place where they found piled belongings was along a breakfront in the living room out front. There were stacks of books, periodicals and papers piled high. There was a reading nook set up next to the fireplace in the room; a overstuffed armchair, reading lamp and small table were tucked cozily off to the side of the mantle.

"Looks like she missed something," Myra said from the entranceway as Barry went back into the room. She pointed at the small tea service set on the table beside the chair.

As soon as he entered the room, Barry's. stomach rolled and the chill fused through him. He stepped over to the table and removed the cover from the teapot. "Well, there's no mold or anything. I'll bet this was one of the last places in the house she was in." He couldn't understand it. This room was the most uncomfortable in the house, but Stella seemed to set up shop here with all her books and papers.

"Hey, get a load of this," he said, pointing to a object next to the entranceway. Myra leaned forward and craned her neck.

She chuckled. "Looks like something from Dora The Explorer."

Barry stepped over to the huge globe set in a stand. It was almost three feet across and was mounted on an elaborate wooden stand. He peered at the surface. "This is an antique," he said. "The countries outlined on the map go back before the first world war." He gave it a spin. "Well, what's up with this?"

"What?" asked Myra. "Tell me. I'm not setting foot in there if I can help it, Barry." She looked up at the ceiling and back to her husband. "This room's weird."

"There's a couple of lines painted on the surface. One's white and the other's black." He spun the globe. "There's a few others… but these two… hmmm…"

"What's with the 'hmmm… professor?"

He looked up. He'd be moving all these books *and* this globe over to the dining room or kitchen, for sure. His curiosity was going crazy. He rested a finger on the globe. "The black and white lines… they intersect right where Kingston would show on the globe."

****

The next day, Barry sat at the dining table in the old limestone house, surrounded on each side with books and papers. The first thing he did when he came in was move her stuff out of the living room and into the dining room. He'd tried sitting in Stella's old chair in the living room where a the books were set out but somehow it didn't feel right. The chair was comfortable enough but the room was cold and his stomach was a hard lump in his body. The feeling that he wasn't alone in there had made his skin tighten and the hair on his arms prickle.

There was no law that said he had to work in there.

It would be a slog going through all of it but there was no way he wanted anything that might have been meaningful to Stella, or even *now* to him and Myra, going to a Goodwill store.

The previous night he and Myra decided that they would take up residency as soon as possible to get the clock ticking for the money and deed. She was at the apartment sorting through stuff for the big move. He had begged off so he could come back here alone and sort through Stella's stuff.

He wussed out telling Myra about what Stella had said about the house in the video; they both had a laugh about how they'd have to feng shui the living room and he left it at that. A crappy front room in a house this huge was no big deal, right?

After a few trips to the dining room, his arms laden with the old books and papers, he was ready to begin. When he reached for the first book, it slipped from his grasp, almost as if his hand had been jostled. The heavy tome landed with a thud on the tiled floor. His eyes flickered to the right and left, but there was only himself in the large, bright room.

He took a deep breath and bent to pick it up but the cover of the book next in the tower caught his eye. It had a colourful picture of the earth, and was titled

'Ley Lines and Places of Energy'. His eyes opened wide and for a moment it felt like his fingertips tingled.

'Places of power...hallowed ground', Stella's words drifted through his mind. This was one that he'd need to read.

The tower of books next to him was huge and he let out a slow sigh. There were so many to go through and it was late in the day. He started to set the book into the 'keeper' pile but his hand came to a halt. An unseen force held the book in his grip.

The smell of lilacs drifted in the air and he felt an overpowering sense of Stella. From the corner of his eye the lace curtain hanging at the side of the wide window, fluttered. He turned his head, peering hard at it, watching it slow down and then stop.

There was no doubt he was meant to read that book sooner, rather than later.

His thumb slid over the edges of the page and closing his eyes, he flipped the book open somewhere near the middle of it. If Stella wanted him to read a certain section, then the randomness of finding it like that, was as good a way as anything else. A paragraph was highlighted, the yellow lines wavy, with a penned asterisk in the margin.

"...that a grid of magnetic energy lines circle the earth. Places such as Stonehenge, the Pyramids and the Great Wall of China are positioned on these lines.

52

In the 1800's many people in the British Isles sensed the energy of these lines and thought them to be 'fairy paths' connecting certain hilltops. Furthermore, it was a dangerous business for a wayward traveler to walk these paths."

Barry's forehead furrowed as he read. This had to be what Stella had referred to in the videotape—the hallowed ground was really 'ley lines of power'. He flipped to the next page and once more his reading began where she had highlighted.

"More spiritual and paranormal activity is said to occur on these lines, with the power amplified where two ley lines intersect. Certain people sensitive to paranormal activity report low-frequency vibrations on the skin and sensations of dizziness and unbalance."

Barry sat back in the chair and closed the book. He'd felt the tingle on the back of his neck, and sensed the old lady's presence. Was this the way it would be from now on? If what he'd just read was true, Stella had known and chosen him over a blood relative to live in this space--a house centered on a ley line.

There was more to this than she'd let on. Why did it have to be someone with the 'second sight' who had to live there? He stood up and plucked the package of sticky notes from his shirt pocket, peeling one off and placing it on top of the pile of books. He'd keep these books and go through them later when they moved in. He'd have more time then.

A thud from the living room made him jump. Shit! It had been really loud. His heart beat harder as he strode through the kitchen and library, to enter the dimly lit front room. Everything looked the way it had when he'd left it earlier. He walked over to the window and peered outside. There was only the yard and the laneway where his cab was parked, no sign of anyone or anything.

Next to the car was an old apple tree, the trunk gnarled and twisted, bare of leaves but... His eyes opened wider when he looked closer and saw the flock of crows crowded together on every branch, their beady eyes watching him. There had to be at least a *hundred* of them!

The sight made his stomach roil and for a moment his knees turned to jelly. Their presence was ominous. Even if he'd never seen that old Alfred Hitchcock movie, *'The Birds'*, he would have known that. If there was any force or power that was trying to scare him off, they had picked the right weapon.

He *hated* birds with their quick movements and lice ridden feathers. He was even repelled by the colourful ducks and swans that swam along the city's nature trail.

He closed the curtain and took a deep breath. Stella wanted him here. It had been so important to her that she'd sweetened the deal with the promise of half a million dollars at the end of a year. There was no way any stupid birds were going to derail that, especially not with a baby on the way.

He smirked and his voice held a trace of defiance. "Is that all you got, buddy?"

Buddy? Yeah. Instinctively he knew the malignant force was male.

A half hour later, he stepped outside and looked up at the apple tree. Nothing there now except a few leaves that refused to succumb to the winds of November. He locked the front door and when he turned to go to the car, a dark shape under the living room window caught his attention. He took a few steps closer and stopped. It was a dead crow; the head angled oddly to the side. That had to be the noise from earlier, a thud on the glass when the bird had flown into it and broke its neck.

His grimaced, walking over to get into the car. With any luck, some stray cat or racoon would find it and haul it off for a snack. He slid in behind the wheel and turned the key in the ignition. When he twisted to watch the laneway, to back out, his head jerked back seeing what lay on the front passenger seat.

His mouth went completely dry as he stared at it. The book on Ley Lines and Power that he'd been reading inside lay open on the seat next to him.

Chapter 6

When Barry wandered into the master bedroom, Myra was bent over, tucking the sheets under the mattress. She was a petite sprite, with strong and shapely legs, a fact that the tight black leggings did nothing to hide. Sunshine through the window highlighted the reddish glints in her hair when she straightened. She looked over her shoulder at him and cast a grin.

"Enjoying the view, you letch?" She flipped her honey blond hair and batted her Betty Boop blue eyes.

He stepped over to her. She wasn't runway model gorgeous, more movie star striking. There was something about her that made people react and do a double take when she walked into a room. It was the confidence in her wide-set large eyes, or maybe her rich full lips twitching in a smile that bordered on sassy. He shook his head at the number of times guys gave him the 'way to go, bud' nod in bars when they were dating.

"You're not done in here, *yet*?" He ducked to the side, dodging the pillow that she hurled at him.

"Whadayamean! I'm not the lazy lout standing around gawking, watching me work!" She laughed when he stepped towards her, scooping her up off her feet, the two of them falling onto the mattress.

He nibbled the hollow of her neck, a spot he knew she found both ticklish and erotic, breathing her floral scented skin. His hands pinned hers to the bed and he continued kissing her.

She nudged her head against his. "Barry! Stop! Your *father* and my *brother* are downstairs moving stuff into the house! What would they say if—"

"I know, I know...you're right...but I can't help myself." He laughed when her leg lifted high enough to kick his butt with her heel, all the while squirming under him.

"Seriously, Barry! Stop!" But her narrow eyes and wide grin were anything but serious.

He released her hands and his fingers slid down her arm, to come to rest on the soft flannel covered mound of her tummy. "I love you, Myra. It's really starting to sink in...we have a home." He shifted and his face was poised above her tummy, "Isabella. It's your Daddy talkin' here. Do you think Mommy should quit slacking off, laying around in bed?"

Myra gave the back of his head a sharp cuff. "Isabella's on my side on this one." She giggled. "She knows the hand that feeds her."

He scoffed. "Hand?"

"Actually, it's the placenta, then it will be a breast—"

"Mmmm…" he said, diving down again.

"Stop it!" she slapped the back of his head. "There won't be any hand feeding of Isabella for quite some time. For now, placenta."

He looked up at her. "Placenta? Ewww."

"Also called the after-birth, y'know."

He blanched and sat up on the bed. "Super eeeew."

She laughed. "Some cultures feed it to the mother, you know. In fact, most mammals, when the female gives birth, eat it afterward."

"Stop."

She leaned into him. "C'mon Barry, this is Bio 101 and Anthropology 101!" She popped him on the shoulder with a fist. "In faaact… some cultures *make the father eat it*! To regain his potency which he lost when he made the baby!"

Barry stood. "I'm gonna be sick here…"

Myra lay back, laughing.

He sighed and shook his head. "Guess I'd better go downstairs and help out." Before he went through the doorway, he turned and winked at her, speaking softly. "But tonight my dear, we christen the house, if ya know what I mean."

His feet beat a fast staccato on the stairs and down into the front hallway. A gust of icy air blew in from the open door where his father and Myra's brother, Tony, were carrying a golden pine desk into the house.

His father's dark eyes looked over at him. "I think we'll get snow later today. I don't like the looks of that grey bank of clouds on the horizon." The older man's fingers looked cold and stiff hooked on the edge of the desk.

"Arthur-ites making a visit, Pop?" Barry asked.

Dad let his end of the desk drop down and rubbed his gnarled hands. "Just a bit, yeah."

Barry watched his father. The man was barely sixty, but had really aged in the last few years. When the plant they both worked at was shut down and moved to Mexico, at least Pop had enough time in to be able to take early retirement. But the last five years had aged him terribly.

Dad looked around the house, shaking his head slowly. "Y'know, kid, you're the best investment I ever made." He turned to his son and smiled.

Pop was right. He lent Barry the start up money to get his taxi and all the other stuff he needed. Barry paid him back quickly; just as they agreed. But if Barry hadn't been a full time driver, he would never have met Stella… He folded his arms and looked at his Dad with love. "Y'know, I got a line on some swampland in Florida…"

Dad waved him off. "I'll take a pass. Take it up with the Koch brothers maybe."

"Yeah. Right."

"Y'know, son," Dad stepped around the desk. Tony stood by silently watching the exchange. "Your mother would be thrilled to see you moving into this place too." He patted Barry's shoulder. "You've always… *always* were a good boy… and a good man. I'm glad that old lady saw it in you too." He turned again admiring the burnished woodwork and craftsmanship of the house.

Mom. The guilt of that day washed over him in a wave. He had kept silent about it since the day she died. He just stared at the floor.

Myra's brother Tony, broke the silence. "Hey, this is the last piece, Barry. Where do you want it?"

Barry grabbed the end of the desk his Dad had been handling. "Down the hall here," they went down the hallway past the living room. He was going to make this his study or something. Maybe he'd write a book based on his experiences driving a cab. They brought in the desk and put it against the wall it shared with the living room.

As they carried the desk, his father closed the front door and then walked slowly behind them. "Lucky the old lady left it furnished. You'd have a hard time filling this place up, son."

"Lucky! I'd say Barry's got a horseshoe stuck up his ass! Talk about luck of the Irish!" Tony flashed a grin and turned to navigate past the furniture in the living room.

Behind him, Barry's Dad continued. "Do ya suppose this fireplace works?" The clang of the brass doors covering the dark hole in the brick sounded. "Let me see...what's this?" The sound of metal scraping against metal, could be heard.

Barry and Tony continued into the small room that overlooked the back yard, now empty of everything but the shelves on the walls, filled with Stella's books. Myra had put her foot down and had them taken out of the dining room.

"Well, looky here!"

Barry set the desk down next to the wall and turned to see his father warming his hands in front of the low, gas-fired flame. The old man shuddered and his face was lined with concern. "I don't know what it is about this room...there's a draft or something." He forced a smile. "You're gonna need this fireplace, if you spend any amount of time in *here*."

"You got that right, George! That makes it much more cozy." Tony stepped into the living room and stood next to Barry's Dad. "Well, it's the north side of the house. It's bound to be colder and the fire helps but..." He smiled. "If it were me, I'd spend all my time in the kitchen and dining room. There's a cheery feel to those rooms. They're brighter."

Barry's hand rose to massage the back of his neck, where his muscles had tensed up. Even his Dad and Tony *felt* the different vibes in the living room and library, and they didn't have the touch. Whatever energy dominated this side of the house was by no means welcoming.

Footsteps on the stairs caused them all to turn and see Myra pop into view. "Who's hungry? I thought I'd go get a pizza or some subs." She grinned and wandered into the room, her eyes wide with pleasure. "Wow! That fireplace actually works?"

Barry watched her sidle up next to his father, vying for the heat.

63

"I'll go. You guys stay here and enjoy a break." Barry stopped in the archway and looked back, shooting them a grin. "But you'll have to put up with my choice for lunch. I say we have pizza."

When he stepped outside, he pulled the collar of his coat higher against the November chill and the blustery damp air. He glanced up at the apple tree and felt relief seeing only the bare branches.

He was about to get into the car when he spotted a tall man standing at the end of the laneway staring at him. The dark overcoat and big hulking body were familiar and his stomach grew tight. Shit. It was Gordon Braithwaite, the son of a bitch from the lawyer's office.

Barry took a deep breath, squaring his shoulders while he walked down the gravelled drive. "What do you want?" Gordon stepped closer and Barry held up his hand. "That's far enough. You're trespassing right now." It was a line he'd never thought he'd ever be able to say, not on a cabbie's pay. He was filled with dark glee being able to say them to this bastard.

And he was a bastard. Barry had loosened the restraints on his touch as soon as he recognized Gordon and had been rewarded with a psychic stench from this jerk.

Gordon's hands were thrust deep inside the pockets of the old, wool coat, and a knitted hat covered

64

his head. His eyes were narrow, shooting glowering daggers at Barry. "That house should be mine! I'm her *blood*. What the hell did you do to the old bat to con her out of this place?"

Barry stepped closer, into Gordon's space. Even though Barry was tall, he still had to look up into the man's eyes. And he was a *lot* bulkier. Barry felt especially skinny going toe to toe with this jerk. Even so, from the flinch back of his head, Gordon wasn't used to people standing up to him.

Gordon was the big fish in a small pond—a prison filled with small-time hoods and punks. The understanding flashed through Barry's brain in a micro-second. Gordon was a bully through and through.

Barry's voice was an ominous hiss. "Get lost, jerk. If I catch you lurking around here again, I'll call the cops." There would be times that Myra would be at the house on her own and this thug—

Oh my God! Barry faltered a step backward as a picture of Gordon beating Myra, dragging her by the hair on her head flashed in his mind. She was a matchstick compared to this monster. And the jerk had no right being there, spying on them while they moved into the house.

A blast of icy wind blew Gordon's knit scarf up, slapping against his jowly cheeks and eyes. For a moment the old hulk faltered.

Barry's eyes opened wider and his body tingled. His eyes focused on the waves of sickly pea green emanating from Gordon's body. It pulsed and hovered making Gordon's face grow dimmer in the sickening hues.

Barry gasped. He knew he was seeing this guy's aura, but he had never seen an aura before. He clenched his fists and growled at the man. "Get in your car and leave here. Your father and his brood were cut off from Evelyn's estate years and years ago. You have *no* claim." As soon as the words were out of his mouth, Barry's head jerked back. What the hell? He didn't know any Evelyn or anything at all about Stella's family!

But he knew he was right.

His words also knocked the stuffing out of Gordon. For a moment his mouth fell open and then snapped shut. His eyes were narrow and spittle formed in the corner of his thick lips when he spoke. "She told you that? Lies, all lies. The old bat was senile and you played her! Jails are filled with con artists like you!" But Gordon had stepped back and was turning to go back to the street even as he spat his insults.

Barry stood his ground watching Gordon walk out of the laneway and then disappear. With every breath, his body became heavier and heavier. His vision blurred for a few seconds and he blinked fast to clear it.

The surge of energy was gone, replaced by a heaviness weighing down his muscles.

He turned and walked back down the laneway to his cab. The screech of a bird overhead made him startle and look up. There in the apple tree, a lone crow, black and shining as obsidian, flapped its wings, its beady eyes watching him with malice.

Chapter 7

Two weeks later...

Myra took the pot off the stove and glanced out the window over the sink. The snow was still falling in fat, sleepy flakes, blanketing the back yard in a pristine slumber. She poured the ginger tea mix through a strainer, taking a deep breath of the spicy steam to clear her sinuses. She picked the mug up and wandered over to the old, wooden table to take a seat there.

Much as she hated being sick and missing work, the moment was comfortingly self-indulgent, relaxing in the quiet of their house. The snow storm just added to the sense of cozy hibernation. Now, if only Barry didn't have to drive that day, ferrying Christmas shoppers or people not wanting to drive the snow covered roads.

She blew her nose and tossed the tissue into the waste basket. Her fingers flew on the keys of her laptop. This would be the extent of her Christmas shopping, searching and typing instead of trudging along with the other hordes at the mall. She had a pretty good idea what to get her brother and his kids, but Barry was still a mystery. Page after page of gift ideas filled the screen and she became lost in the web of items.

A heavy bang in the front of the house sounded and she jerked upright. Barry was home? Quick as anything, she snapped the laptop shut. She'd have to wait until Barry left again before going back to shopping. After a couple of minutes sitting quietly waiting for him to appear, her eyebrows drew together. It had sounded like the front door closing, but what was he doing?

She wandered slowly through the dining room. "Barry? Is that you?"

Footsteps sounded on the floor above, walking across the hallway and then a door closed with a shuddering bang. She hurried through the room and glanced at the entrance looking for his coat or winter boots. Nothing there. A frown creased her forehead when she looked to the right up the stair case.

She stepped quickly up the stairs. "Barry?" There were four rooms on the upper level, a large master bedroom taking up most of one side of the house next to the bathroom, while two smaller bedrooms were on the opposite side. The doors to the small bedrooms were always shut to conserve heat but their bedroom and the bathroom door were open. She peeked into the bathroom, only to find the room empty save for the claw-foot bathtub, toilet and pedestal sink.

Pulling the heavy fleece bathrobe snug to her body, she stepped into the bedroom. The whimsical crazy patchwork quilt on the bed was a sharp contrast to the deep unease that was settling in her chest. Again, there was no one there in the room.

She stood silently looking around for any sign of what had caused the thud. But really, it was the footsteps that really creeped her out.

Who is up here?

She should call Barry. But the cell phone was down on the kitchen table. Her breath was ragged in her throat and she clutched the robe even tighter still.

After risking a peek out the crack of the bedroom door, she raced down the stair and into the kitchen. Her hands shook, clicking the phone on and tapping his name in the contact list. She gripped it tightly in her hand, cursing as the ringtone buzzed once, twice...in steady rhythm. There was no way she was staying in the house, not if someone was upstairs hiding. She raced to the front hallway and thrust her feet into her winter boots.

"Hello?"

"Barry! I think there's someone in the house. I heard footsteps upstairs!" Her words were rushed, trying to hold the phone to her ear and shrug her arms into her winter coat.

"I'm two minutes away."

"Hurry! I'm going outside and walking to the street. I'll watch for you." She clicked the phone off and her hand was a flash pulling the front door open and striding out. In the stillness of the snow, it seemed surreal, her feet ploughing briskly through the drifts up the laneway. Had she really heard someone or could it have been something outside?

She shook her head. No way. That was definitely someone walking across the second floor. She was physically sick, not mentally, and even that was just a cold. After a few minutes she was on the sidewalk, looking back at the house for any sign of life, any movement in the window.

Cars driving slowly by on the slippery streets made the falling snow swirl around her body, almost obliterating her view of anything but whiteness. At the sharp blare of a car horn she turned and saw the white cab lumber slowly into the laneway. When he stopped, she pulled the passenger door open and got into the warm interior.

"You okay?"His eyes were wide with concern peering at her.

"I'm fine! Scared as hell, but I'll survive." Her heart pounded hard in her chest and she tried to catch her breath. "It sounded like the front door closed and then there were footsteps upstairs. I thought it was you! When I went up, I checked our bedroom and the bathroom."

"Not the other two bedrooms, right?" His face was a mask of worry mixed with anger.

"Are you kidding! No way." She shook her head. This was too much for them to handle alone. "We should call the police."

He looked to the side at the drifts of snow mounting higher in the driveway. "Were there any footprints in the snow when you walked up the lane?"

She'd been so scared, she'd never thought of that. Were there any other marks or footprints besides hers? She couldn't be sure. But even so, maybe the prowler came around the house from the back yard. "Barry, I'm scared. We should call—"

"No. I know what the problem is." He sighed and put the car in gear, inching slowly up the driveway

72

to the house. He clicked his seatbelt off and turned to her. "Stay in the car."

"No way! I've got my phone and you're not going in there alone. I'll stay by the door with my finger on 911 ready to press it." She opened the door and looked over at him after she got out. "What do you think it is?"

He looked uncomfortable, looking down at the ground for a moment and then he let out a long sigh. His eyes met hers. "The house is haunted."

Chapter 8

It didn't register with her at all. She looked up into his eyes as if he had just spoken in Klingon.

"The who is what?"

Shit. This wasn't going to go well. At. All. "The house." He dropped his head and stared at the toes of his boots. "It's sort of haunted."

Myra grabbed his open coat. "Barry! This isn't funny! There's a burglar upstairs!" With a scoff, she let go and went to her phone pressing buttons. "I'm calling the cops!"

"No, Myra, they'll think you're crazy," he said, keeping his voice calm.

She stopped what she was doing and looked up at him. "*I'm* crazy? You're kidding, right? I heard someone break in and go upstairs! *You're* the one saying Casper's come for a visit!"

He put his arm around her and turned her towards the driveway and street beyond. With his other hand, he pointed. "Look. There's your footprints going out to the sidewalk." He moved his finger. "Those are the only footprints."

She looked up at him again. "You're *serious*?"

The shocked look in her eyes told him he'd really screwed up. He should have told her *everything* about the house earlier. It was just that he'd wanted this so bad, and he thought he could handle it without involving or upsetting her. "I didn't think you needed to know..."

"You never thought I *needed* to know?" Her jaw thrust forward and her lips pressed tight together. She huffed a loud breath that plumed before her face in the frosty air, hiding it for a moment.

"Myra...I'm sorry. I should have told you."

The thump of her fist giving him a hard swat on the arm was well deserved. "Asshole! I was scared shitless earlier..." She shook her head and looked down at the step, "Frig! I'm still scared! But now I know it's just..." Her fingers made quotation marks next to her face. "...'ghosts'—something you didn't think was important enough to mention!"

He dropped his head again and scuffed some snow with his toe. "I'm sorry."

"Whose ghost, Barry?" She slapped at his chest again. "Was someone murdered in this place? Is that why the living room feels so weird?"

He lifted his head and stepped to the door to pull it open. How could he have ever thought he'd be able to keep something like this from Myra? She was smart as a whip. She could finish a cross word puzzle in ten minutes while he struggled to get even the first clue.

"Let's go inside. It's freezing out here and you've already got a cold." He lifted his hand to guide her inside but she brushed it away like a gnat.

"Don't touch me." She slipped by him and ripped the winter coat away from her body.

He just barely missed getting hit on the shin by one of the boots she kicked off. Wow! He'd never seen her *this* mad at him. His stomach slumped lower to the floor watching the whites rim the blue of her irises. She was scared too.

He held his hands before him and looked softly at her. "Stay here, Myra, while I check this out. We'll talk afterwards, I promise."

He slipped his winter boots off and ducked into the living room to get the iron fireplace poker. Better safe than sorry. But, it wouldn't be a person... well, a physical person anyway; he'd bet his life on that one.

76

Myra stood with her arms crossed over her chest near the door but she purposely kept her eyes from meeting his gaze.

He took the stairs two at a time, brandishing the poker like a sword before him. When he reached the top step, it was just as she'd said. The doors to the bathroom and their bedroom were open but the other two doors across the hallway were shut tight. The hair on the back of his neck rose and he felt a chill when he stepped forward to open the first bedroom door.

But what he saw made his eyes pop wide. His hand hung frozen in the air as he watched the knob turn all on its own, slowly, making a low, scraping sound. He pulled back and when the door whooshed open and banged hard against the wall behind it, he almost jumped out of his skin

Myra's voice broke the silence. "Barry? What's happening?"

Her footsteps pounded up the stairs and he spun around to face her. "Stay there!"

He stepped into the room, and his breath formed a white vapour. The room was way too cold. They'd closed it off to save heat but this chill was like stepping into the vegetable room at Costco.

His knees started knocking as he looked around the room. The thought of going past the bed and inspecting the closet made his skin crawl. Somehow, he

77

knew in his gut that the room was like a black hole in space, threatening to suck the life-force and energy from his body. He shouldn't be in there!

'Don't be afraid. You are stronger.' Stella's calm voice in his head caught him by surprise.

His eyes darted back and forth around the room. Stronger than what? He took a deep breath and feeling just slightly more confident, he inched forward.

His mouth fell open seeing the flickering band of light under the closet door. "What the...?"

He grabbed the door handle and yanked it open. A bare light bulb hung from the ceiling, flashing erratically, the sparks of light losing the battle with darkness as it burned out.

He reached to pull the chain attached to the fixture, extinguishing the last glimmer. Every muscle in his body was alert and energized, his movements stiff when he shut the closet door. He turned and gasped, coming to a complete stop.

A shimmering shape hovered next to the window. He blinked a couple times to clear his eyes, making sure the afterimage of the light wasn't playing tricks with his vision.

The image was of a young woman in a dark dress with white lace at the cuffs of her sleeves. Her eyes were blue white and her face pale and ethereal.

She nodded to him and without a word, lifted a translucent hand The lightness of her being turned shades of pink and blue and then faded from sight.

Like the day that Stella had died—was this the woman in the window he'd seen? Yeah, it had been this window!

Stella's voice was in his head again. *'Be at peace, Barry. Evelyn's with us as well.'*

"Who the hell is Evelyn?" his voice came out in a soft whisper. But the sense of Stella had evaporated.

"Barry! What's going on?" This time, Myra's voice was urgent.

He turned and left the room, closing the door behind him. Myra had taken a few steps higher, gripping the handrail with ivory knuckles.

He walked over to the second bedroom, not expecting to see much of anything. Whatever force had caused the light to turn on and the image of the woman to appear was gone now. He strode into the room and looked around, his heartbeat slowing to a more normal rhythm.

What had that been in the first bedroom? The woman had been so clear that she looked like a living person for a moment, just like the day that Stella had died. It had been shocking but he hadn't felt fear. If a person saw a ghost, shouldn't they feel scared out of their wits? It was weird but that was all. Evelyn. Hmm.

"There's nothing here, Myra. Let's go downstairs." He forced an easy confidence in his voice that he wasn't feeling. This time when he reached to place his arm around her shoulders, she didn't shrug him off.

"This is a bad joke, Barry. It's like the scary stories kids used to tell about people having to spend a night in a haunted house to get a pot of money. Except, for us, it's a year. What kind of crazy, sadistic woman does that to a friend? Stella *was* your friend, right?"

He took a deep breath following her into the kitchen. "She and I are very much alike, Myra." He slipped his coat off and hung it over the back of a chair. He tried to gauge her face as she poured more of the tea mixture into a mug and nuked it. But she was silent, her jaw set tight.

"You know how sometimes, I know things are going to happen before they do, how I can tell if someone's sick or lying. Kind of a sixth sense sort of thing. I try not to think about it, but it's there." He took a seat at the table and folded his hands together on the table, his eyes never leaving Myra.

"You mean your 'touch'." When he nodded, her gaze shifted to meet his for a moment before taking the mug and carrying it over to join him at the table. "Yeah, sure. Like when you insisted we cancel the hotel on our honeymoon and there was that horrible fire. Yeah, I know. You try to fight it but every now and then, it just comes out. Usually it's true." There was still no sign of warmth in her voice.

"We never really talked about it."

"Of course not! That aspect of you always weirded me out, Barry." She pointed a finger at him. "You told me that this 'touch' of yours did more harm than good when you were a kid, right? You're the one who didn't want to discuss it, and that was fine by me."

"Yeah... when I was in the fourth grade, it got really strong, and I showed off at school and got my ass kicked for it." He sighed. "So when I had the vision of my Mom getting into a car wreck, I didn't say anything."

"What are you talking about? A vision of your Mom?"

"The touch had always been with me when I was a kid." He shrugged. "Like I knew what was wrapped up under the tree at Christmas."

"You still know that?"

He nodded.

"What a freaking waste of time and effort wrapping your Christmas presents!"

He shrugged off her attempt at humor. "Anyway, it got really strong with me when I was nine. I was able to *see into* the heads of the kids at school. And the teachers, too." He took a breath. "And the more I used it, the better I got at it." He chuckled. "I was nailing tests and quizzes like there was no tomorrow." A cloud went over his face. "But I took it too far, and started telling some of the kids stuff they really didn't want to hear."

"Like what?"

"Just stupid kid stuff— Jane Charmichal enjoyed teasing her sister's cat, Joey Waco's grandmother really didn't like him..." his voice faded. "And then I told Phil Walsh that he liked guys instead of girls..."

"Oops."

"You're not kidding. He, Joey Waco and some other kids ganged up on me after school." He ran his finger down the side of his nose. "That's when the schnoz got busted, them teaching me a lesson."

She patted his hand. "It gives your face character. Like a Roman gladiator."

"Yeah..." his eyes teared up. "So two days later I had a vision of my Mom getting into a car wreck..." he looked down. "And that time I didn't say anything. I wuss'ed out 'cause I didn't wanna get in trouble!"

82

"Barry!" When his head shot up, she said, "You were *nine years old* and you had just been beaten! Savagely beaten! You had your face kicked in because of these visions! Of course you'd keep quiet!"

"And she died!"

Myra stood and put her arms around him, cradling his head to her bosom. "Barry... Barry... maybe it was her time..." She held him as his shoulders heaved and he sobbed out old grief. "It was *not* your fault..." she repeated softly.

****

When he collected himself, Myra poured him a cup of tea and sat across from him at the table.

"So what *are* we doing here, Barry? Why did Stella leave you this house? What's really going on?"

He looked around the kitchen and felt the tension in the back of his neck fade. Whatever energy field was in this room, it was positive. Everyone who came into the kitchen felt lighter, more relaxed. It was the best place to have this conversation with Myra, that was for sure.

He took a deep breath. "Stella saw the touch in me. She has it too."

"*Had* it, you mean."

He made a sharp smile. "Not exactly." Before Myra could go down *that* road, he hurried on. "This house sits on energy fields." He nodded towards the room he had set up as an office. "All of Stella's books and papers? They all relate to different interpretations of that idea." He made a wry look. "The one she likes the best is where they're called 'Ley Lines'.

Myra gave a short nod. "Yeah, there's a book about that you've been poring over."

He nodded.

"So what are they?"

"I'm not exactly sure. Stella told me that the longer we live here, the clearer it will become."

"Barry, you got to come up with something better than that! It's not just about you, or me now!"

He held up a hand. "I know, I know! Let me tell you what I know, and I'll tell you what I think, okay?"

She pressed her lips together and nodded at him to go on.

"Okay. The best I can figure out, is these lines are positive and negative in nature, and they circle and surround the earth. Things go along pretty much okay when they're in harmony... but... there's a couple of things."

"Wait, wait. What do you mean positive and negative."

84

He shot her a look. "Light. Dark. Love. Hate. Good... and evil. Those are the best approximations we can have as humans." He held his hands out, palms down and laid the edges next to each other. "Think if them like tectonic plates along an earthquake fault line. Where the edges of my hands touch, that's the fault line. As long as the plates are in balance, no problem. But..." He tilted one hand and the other slid under it, causing them to go askew. "If one gains more power it can disrupt the other, and disrupt that balance on the planet."

"And that's not good."

He nodded. "It's happened before according to some research Stella left. These 'fault lines' come and go in areas; they move around. This house sits on one right now, but there were others."

"Oh? Where?"

"New York City on September 11, 2001. Hiroshima Japan when the atomic bomb dropped." He shook his head slowly. "But the biggest one that Stella was able to trace was at a place called Wannasee."

"Where's that?"

"It's the place in Germany where they made it official government policy to annihilate the Jewish race."

Myra jumped to her feet. *"And you're telling me that we're sitting on such a place right now?"*

He nodded. "Yeah, I'm pretty sure we are." He looked around. "Right smack dab in the middle of it. That's why the living room feels weird, but the kitchen feels cozy."

"And we're supposed to stop some kind of paranormal earthquake from happening?"

"Yeah."

"How?"

He shook his head slowly. "That part I don't know."

"You don't know! Jeeeezus!" Myra slapped the table. "Who—no, *what* the hell was it that was upstairs?"

"That was Evelyn. She's here to help."

"You know its name?"

"Well... I was kinda told its name."

"By who?" Myra shot a hand up. "Wait. Don't tell me— *Stella* told you, right?" When she saw him nod she sat down in a huff.

"Evelyn's not here to hurt us. It's a spirit or ghost or some sort of entity." He snorted. "Not to sound too much mysterious but it was from the other. I don't know why it chose today to appear or what it wants but I sensed that it's benevolent."

Her chin fell to her chest and when she looked up there was a wide smirk on her face and her eyes rolled before meeting his. "So it's a woman? This woman...what if she changes her mind? Can she attack us...hurt us? Or is she just looking for shits and giggles, scaring the hell out of us?"

"I didn't sense evil or bad intentions coming from this woman. She's connected— it's someone who once lived here. That much I know."

"How did she manage to... you know... show up?"

"I think that the barrier is weakening between this dimension... this plane of existence... and the other side." He looked Myra in the eye. "Our job is to keep it secure."

"I still don't get it. Why does someone like *you* have to live here?" Her eyes narrowed. "She dangled that carrot--the pot of money at the end--pretty high, if you ask me. I have to share a house with ghosts or whatever likes to be near these power lines for a *year*? An entire *year*?" She shook her head. "The reward doesn't sound all that great, if that's the case."

He rose and walked into the library, returning with the book he knew Stella had meant for him to read. And he had! He understood it, but that didn't mean he could explain it in any way that made sense. He was no professor!

Setting the book, *'Ley Lines and Earth Energy'* in front of her, he once more took a seat. "I put sticky notes on the pages that are important." He watched her pick the book up and open it to the first marked page. "Basically, this house sits on a spot where two of these power lines intersect. It's a place of enormous energy and power. I think..."

He sighed and saw her gaze flicker up to meet his. "...there's a kind of battle going on. The house sits on a vortex of energy which bad entities can use to escape from..." He shook his head and his face was tight. "...from another realm or dimension if you will. We've both felt one side of the house is extremely negative. It's a spot where the veil separating life from death is quite thin."

"A battle? And that ghost woman escaped and she's upstairs in the spare room?" She rolled her eyes once more and her jaw clenched. "That will sure help me sleep better knowing she's just down the hall."

"She's not here to hurt us, Myra!"

"But there are bad ones here. Someplace, right?" Stella looked around the house.

"I haven't felt them."

Myra's eyes drilled into him. "You haven't felt them *yet*."

He nodded in agreement. "But, whatever the hell they are— any of them— they're not as strong as life."He cocked his head and looked up towards the ceiling. "They'll feed on our fear when they come," he said softly. His eyes closed and he shook his head. "Stella told me that, just now."

"What? She *is* here! You can see her?" Myra set the book down and her eyes were wide staring at him.

"Yes, she's here; no, I can't see her. I feel her though. She's here looking out for us. That woman, Evelyn? I saw her in the window of that same bedroom the day Stella died." Even though she lived in the half of the house that was 'the negative side', he knew she wasn't evil. She was trapped or something. She'd even waved at him that day in the cab.

Myra had heard enough. She got up and stood at the kitchen counter, looking out the window at the snow, which was falling harder now. "I don't know, Barry. This is all too spooky and weird. I don't know if I can do this. Not even for all that money."

Barry took a deep breath. "Myra, if you could have prevented 9/11 from happening, and the subsequent shit storm that's been going on since, would you?" Before she could answer, he said, "If you could have prevented the death camps from being built *and used on innocent people* would you?" He leaned back in his chair, knowing he was right. "No, honey, you'd never be able to live with yourself, and you know it. It's not the money... not anymore."

"But why us? Why us, Barry?"

He gave her a sick smile and shrugged his shoulders with vigor. "Why not?"

<u>Chapter 9</u>

Myra stood up and stepped to the window overlooking the back yard. If Barry was right, then the money didn't matter a damn considering the stakes. Millions died in the Nazi death camps, and how many lives had been destroyed since 911?

But.

Tears stung her eyes and her chin quivered. She wanted to believe that everything would work out, that he'd be able to protect her and the baby...but the stakes were too high. There was a *child* growing inside her, a child that she'd never thought they'd ever actually have. They'd lost three babies in early miscarriages, so the odds were already stacked against them.

Isabella...she sniffed hard knowing that the child was a daughter and they'd agreed to name her that. Someone had to be strong and look out for the baby, even if it meant walking away from the house and the money.

What good was money, when the baby's survival as well as their own was at stake? They'd been doing okay before, living in the apartment, pinching pennies. They could go back to that.

Everything weighed down on her shoulders. Plus, she was still fighting the flu, not even able to take any medications for it. She turned into Barry and wiped the tears from her cheeks. "I need to lay down for a bit." She shook her head and her words were low. "Is it safe to go upstairs?"

Barry's fingers tucked a lock of hair that had fallen forward, behind her ear. His eyes were concerned and sad. "Yes. But I want to go up and stay with you. It might make you feel better."

She nodded, feeling the tension knotting the back of her neck let go. His hand slipped over hers and she let him lead her out of the kitchen and up the stairs. "You sure whatever was up here is gone, that it won't come near us?"

He pulled the duvet back and stepped to the side letting her slip by him. "I would know, Myra. Trust me."

Jerk. His 'trust me' account was pretty, pretty thin; didn't he realize that?

She didn't bother taking the robe off. She just slipped into the soft bed and closed her eyes, snuggling deep under the covers. Normally she could get past the sleepiness of the early stages of the pregnancy. A few deep breathing exercises and a prayer and she'd be good to go. Today however, she couldn't muster the strength.

The other side of the bed depressed and she felt his body laying beside her, still on top of the bedspread. Her eyes closed and she took a deep breath, sinking lower into the cushiony warmth.

****

A high pitched wail sounded. It became louder and more insistent. She startled and her hand jerked to her stomach. The baby. Her eyes fluttered open watching the bedroom door creak open...slowly.

An old woman carrying a baby, swaddled in a white blanket appeared. Silver hair framed an ancient face, while her blue eyes arrested Myra with their startling intensity. The woman's shoulders were narrow and her liver-spotted hands curled over the white, lace trim of the baby blanket, a wan smile on her lips as she walked over to the bed.

Only part of the baby's profile, the curve of its forehead and tip of the nose, could be seen above the edge of the blanket. The cries were like the mewls of a kitten now, becoming fainter and fainter.

Myra sat up higher in the bed and bent her knees forming a cradle with her body. She extended her arms to take the baby.

The elderly lady bent and placed the pink faced infant into Myra's arms. "She's perfect." Her voice was a soft whisper.

Myra's breasts ached with every cry that the baby made. Its tiny fists thrust out of the fleecy covering, making Myra's eyes well with tears. They were so delicate and perfectly formed. The child's head turned into Myra's chest when she held it close, the survival instinct already strong as it sought food. Her daughter.

She glanced up at the old woman. "Where's Barry?" He should be there to share this moment.

The old lady's eyes closed and she shook her head.

In an instant, she knew Barry was dead. A wrenching pain filled Myra's chest, consuming her. She stared at her daughter and hot tears fell from her cheeks onto the blanket. It couldn't be true, but the hollow in her body told her otherwise. Her sobs wracked her shoulders and she held the baby closer, her voice a soft keen, "No, no, no..."

The old woman's chin rose high. "He succeeded. You and the baby are safe now. But he needed you. Your strength would have saved him." She turned and walked over to the door, holding the edge of it in her gnarled fingers. "Good bye, my dear."

Myra's looked over at her. Her mouth was suddenly dry and heart was beating fast in her chest. She tried to speak, to cry out to the old woman— *'Don't go! Stay with me! Help me and the baby!'*—but nothing came out. Her mouth was full of cotton, the words stuffed deep in her throat.

The door inched and there was a low snick as the latch caught. She was alone in the world. Alone with the baby. Barry had saved her, even when she had been too scared to save him. The tears continued to flood the pillow under her cheek.

****

"Myra." A nudge and the gentle voice was next to her ear.

She didn't want to open her eyes, didn't want to face life this way. She pulled the blanket higher over her cheek.

"C'mon, Myra. Wake up. You're having a bad dream."

Oh my God! It was Barry's voice! Her eyes flew open and she looked at him with sleepy wonder, her cheeks still damp with tears.

He handed her a glass of water and smiled. "After you fell asleep I went downstairs to get the book. I was going to come back up and read it laying here with you. I thought I'd bring some water for when you woke up. But you were moaning when I came back into the room."

He sat on the edge of the bed and his eyes were full of love and concern watching her.

Thank God, he was there. Thank God it had only been a dream, a bad dream, but a dream none the less.

She took a sip of the water and sat higher in the bed, her back propped against the headboard. "What did Stella look like, Barry?"

"She was an old woman. What can I say?" He laughed and his hand drifted to her shoulder, giving it a gentle squeeze.

"Men!" She chuckled, suddenly glad that he was there and she could tease him. "What colour were her eyes? Was she tall, short, plump, skinny? You never once described her to me."

He looked down at the coverlet for a few seconds. "She was short, stooped over a bit and rail thin." When he looked back at Myra, there was a warm smile on his lips. "Her eyes were blue. A vivid sky blue which was strange for someone so elderly. Normally there's a light pall to an old person's eyes, but not hers.

To the day she died she was sharp eyed. Why do you ask?"

Myra's body was light, alive with relief and excitement. When she'd come to bed she'd had the weight of the world on her shoulders but now... "I dreamed about her. She was exactly like you just described. And Barry?"

His head pulled back and above the smile there was happiness and awe in his eyes. "Yeah?"

Her hand slipped over his and it felt so right. The two of them together, always. "She handed our baby girl to me. Oh Barry!" Tears once more pooled in her eyes and her voice hitched. "Isabella was beautiful. Her tiny face and hands were perfect. I wish you'd seen her."

He slid his hand under the covers and onto her tummy. "I will, Myra." He leaned over and kissed her cheek, lingering there and speaking softly. "If there was any other way, I'd jump at it. But we need to be here. It's not the money or even the house. There's something far more important at stake here."

She didn't need a sixth sense to know that what he said was true. She loved and trusted him. That was the most important thing. They were a family who loved each other above anything else.

Love would be their weapon. Her arms rose and she hugged him closer still, the two of them basking in the shared moment.

Neither of them heard the growl and the high feline shriek from the cellar two floors below.

Chapter 10

Later that day, Barry was in the study sorting through the books that Stella had left. He had tackled this job a bit at a time, reading ones that caught his eye...actually ones that he knew Stella had wanted him to read first. The imprint of her essence still clung to the old books like the faded scent of flowers, stronger in some than in others. Sure enough, when he opened the 'strong' ones, he found many pages that she'd highlighted with the yellow marker.

The room's 'atmosphere' was still negative, but at a lower ebb right now. He didn't know why; maybe the bad guys were on a break. He found the concept of malevolent entities from another dimension having work rules kind of funny. At any rate, he wasn't going to concede any part of their home for free.

Snippets of music drifted into the room from the kitchen where Myra sat at the table, reading the 'Ley

Line' book and sipping tea. Soon, he would get up and start making dinner for them.

A scratching sound caught his attention and his head dipped to the side, cocking his ear. Was it the music or had there been something? Again, the scratch...coming from the door under the staircase, the one leading to the cellar.

His stomach tightened thinking of that place. He'd only been down there once to check it out and couldn't get out of there fast enough. The air down there was musty and damp from the earthen floor and dank limestone block walls but there was more...it was like something down there was watching him, ready to pounce at any minute. And what that something might be made his skin crawl.

This time the scratch was louder and there was a faint, mewling sound. He got up and walked by the kitchen, glancing at his wife but purposely not interrupting her reading. She was intent on the book, which was a good thing. Together the two of them would figure all of this out. It would take team work and Myra was wicked smart.

He frowned turning the knob to the basement door. This time, it wasn't a scary feeling flooding his body, just one that was high on the nuisance factor.

The door was only open a few inches when something streaked by his legs, hissing. Pure white hair bristled in a curved arch on its back, the tail swishing rapidly from right to left when it stopped at the archway leading to the kitchen. Emerald eyes met Barry's, while its ears were flattened level with the top of its head.

"Here kitty, kitty..." He took a step towards it only to see it dart away to hide behind Myra's legs.

Myra set the book down and leaned over the edge of the table. "Hello... What have we here?"

From where he stood, Barry could see the cat's tail twitching back and forth and its eyes blink slowly, unsure about Myra's hand coming closer and closer to it.

How the devil had the cat got into the basement? He'd never noticed an outside door.

"Poor thing..." Myra stood up and her slippers hissed on the wooden floor as she walked over to the cupboard and plucked a bowl from the shelf. The light from the fridge flashed and she turned with the milk jug in hand, pouring some into the bowl.

Once more she stepped over to the table and squatted down on her haunches, setting the dish on the floor. Her blue eyes were narrow with mirth watching the cat edge out from its sheltered safety.

"What a pretty kitty." She glanced up at Barry and her eyebrows drew together. "How'd it get in, do you suppose?"

The cat rose to its feet and walked slowly to the bowl of milk, taking a few tentative laps before sinking lower and licking with gusto. It even let Myra, stroke the fur on its head.

"There must a hole in the wall or something, where it got in. I'm not sure. I don't think Stella had a cat. This one must be a stray who came in out of the storm."

Myra shifted so that she sat crossed legged, Indian style on the floor, petting the cat while it ate. The robe had slipped open and her knees showed above the curve of her calf and thick white ankle socks. Even though she was pushing thirty, she looked like a teenager, excited by the cat's sudden appearance.

She smiled and looked up at Barry. "I never had a pet growing up. My brother Tony was allergic to dog and cat dander so we never bothered." She shrugged and once more her hand was drawn to the cat's head. "Never thought they were all that useful anyways, but..." She looked down at the cat, tickling the area under its ear. "...this one's kind of cute."

Barry squatted down next to her and reached for the cat to stroke its back. The cat looked up at him and shifted so that it was closer to Myra. He pulled his hand back and chuckled. "I guess the cat thinks you're pretty cute too. It seems to have taken a shine to you."

The cat looked up and its pink tongue rolled over its whiskers, green eyes blinking slowly and staying softly narrow. It edged closer to Myra and climbed into her lap, rubbing its head against her arm.

Myra giggled and her fingers rubbed the cat's cheek. "She's like a little princess." She smiled and her voice took on a haughty British accent, "You may pet me now." She laughed. "The only princess name I can think of is the one from Star Wars. I think we should call her Princess Leia."

Barry laughed and made no attempt to touch the cat. It obviously preferred Myra, so why push it? "So, if no one shows up looking for it or puts poster up, you want to keep it?" Having a cat felt right and in an old house, it might come in useful with mice. Or birds.

The cat didn't look like it belonged to anyone— no collar and its ears were jagged and ripped at the edges. It wasn't thin and emaciated but it looked like it had been on its own and could take care of itself. The fact that it had come from the cellar said something for its character as well. The way it acted, rushing out as soon as it could was in line with Barry's feeling—the cellar wasn't a wonderful place to hang out.

Myra kept petting the cat while she looked over at him and nodded. "Cats are supposed to have a sixth sense. From stories I've heard, they can sense ghosts and weird stuff. It might be good to have it around for

103

when you're working and I'm here all alone...or not alone, if you know what I mean."

Barry watched the cat drift off to sleep and heard the steady rumble of a purr in its throat. It was quite content to adopt them it seemed. The fact that Myra had had the dream about Stella and then the cat showing up was no coincidence. It was meant to be part of the team.

Chapter 11

Gordon Braithwaite kept to the narrow foot path leading to the electricity and water meters. It was late enough in the evening that the loser cabbie and his bitch were in for the night. His teeth ground together while his breath plumed in the frosty air. These people were squatters! Squatters in a house that should have been *his* by rights. *He* was the only blood heir.

Blood is thicker than water. *'And blood will tell...'* He stopped dead in his tracks. The thought that popped into his head... it sounded *powerful*. He gave himself a quick nod and continued his careful slinking down the path.

He took the same spot he'd stood in a few nights earlier, blending into the dark branches of a spruce tree at the corner of the house, with a perfect line of sight into the kitchen window. He was easily able to see the bitch cross the kitchen, her golden hair tied back in a pony tail above collar of her blue robe. Well...wasn't that just so cozy? All warm and snuggled in for the night. Snuggled in *his* goddamn house while he was standing outside, freezing his ass!

Watching the young bitch promenade around the kitchen reminded him a little of 'Aunt' Stella. He had watched the crone from this vantage point regularly for quite some time. It had become his hobby, watching Stella and relishing the warmth of anger in his gut.

That old bitch Stella, had been batshit crazy, choosing to live all alone in this place when she could have sold it and made a fortune. When he was a kid still living at home, he overheard his parents talking about how she had turned down a huge offer from some developer.

Stella was his father's aunt, and as far as the old man was concerned, she could do whatever she wanted with the place. There was no way Dad wanted anything to do with *that* house. What a fool. He tried to find out more from Dad, but whatever it was that he knew went with him to the grave.

When his Mom died, it meant that he was Stella's last living relative. He started sucking up to her on the day of the funeral five years ago.

"You're the only family I have left, Aunt Stella," he mumbled through his tears. "I hope we can be close. I don't want you to be all alone in the world."

"Oh really?" she had peered up at him with a look of disdainful curiosity. She gave a short nod and asked how the disciplinary action was going at work.

His jaw dropped and his head whipped back. "How the hell did you hear about that?" He had squeezed an inmate's balls so hard during a 'routine frisk' that the idiot got a rupture. It was his eighth time getting jammed up and the administration now had a hard-on for him.

The bitch smiled in a coy way. Well, as coy as an old bag could manage. Still her eyes watched him with bright interest when she invited him to her home the following evening.

He'd never forget that visit! It was really odd...right out of the *Twilight Zone*. She'd made tea and served cookies but instead of sitting in the kitchen, like you'd do with family, she insisted that they sit in the living room. At first it had put him off, being treated like some stranger or an insurance salesman but the living room was nice. He'd sat near the fireplace, feeling the warmth and...something else. He couldn't describe the sensation of the surge he'd felt, sitting in that room, but it had been wonderful.

All the while her beady little eyes watched his every move. When he settled into the armchair with a purr of comfort, her face sparked and she nodded to herself. And the questions she'd asked him! It was more

107

like an interrogation than anything resembling a conversation. What was his childhood like, did he have many friends, any pets...all the way up to how he felt about the inmates he saw every day at work.

To make matters worse, she already knew the answers before she asked the questions. When she asked about his time in high school, she wondered aloud whether that little twirp Jamie Dresden ever forgave him for the time he had stuffed the punk's gym socks in his mouth. When she asked about his inmate abuse case at work, she *knew* it was the eighth time he was up on administration charges.

He ran some bullshit past her on that one, and all she did was go, 'That's some doodle you're running past me, Gordon'.

At the door she told him to never come by again. When he asked why, she turned her head and gazed at the living room from the front foyer. Turning back to him she said, "The living room enjoys your company too much," she said as she closed the front door in his face.

What a batshit crazy thing to say. They were the last words she ever spoke to his face.

He snorted softly, rocking back and forth from his toes to his heels. He must not have passed whatever bullshit test she was giving him because, she practically threw him out just as he was really settling in and starting to enjoy being there.

A quick movement in the window startled him. A white cat suddenly appeared on the sill. The cabbie's wife stepped over to stroke its head, and looked out the glass for a moment. Gordon drew back into the prickly fir branches, even though he knew he was well hidden in the night. The cat's yellow green eyes were focused where he stood; the tip of its tail flickered rhythmically, swishing back and forth.

He shoved his hands into his armpits, trying to shake the chill that had crept into his bones, his eyes never leaving the cat. He swallowed hard. That cat's gaze made him uncomfortable.

It's too cold out... let's go inside. Whoa! The idea sounded so loud in his head it was like someone had spoken to him. Still, it was a good one. His toes were starting to go numb. He eased to the side of the house stepping silently.

Lo and behold, a set of steps leading down to the cellar! He grinned and crept down. A black door was at the bottom. With a sigh he grasped the ancient knob and turned it. Dammit, locked. Screw it, it was really old; he'd just force the stupid thing. He grabbed the knob with both hands and twisted.

The muscles in his arm and neck were tight as he bent to open the lock. He could hardly see in the dim light and from the blinding rage at the situation. Here he was, the *rightful* heir having to break into *his* house on a bitter cold winter night. And even if he did manage to trip the lock, it would only let him in the cellar. There was no guarantee he'd be able to get upstairs.

His hand jerked away from the door and he cocked his ear. There was someone right on the other side of the door whispering! He froze. Standing utterly still, he heard his name! He bent forward to the crack in the door.

'*Gordon...*' followed by something he couldn't catch. He leaned into the door and put his ear next to the vertical slit. "*...yours. The house will be yours.*'

His gaze darted back and forth. Yes. *Finally*, someone who agreed with him! A kindred spirit. He tried to see through the crack, for a light, anything. "Who are you?" he hissed.

"*Your friend. I'll help you.*" Hearing the words, at first Gordon's blood pounded in his ears.

With a soft creak, the door began to open on its own. He jumped back, watching it swing inward.

'*Your house, Gordon. Come in.*' The whispers were louder.

"You're damn right it's mine!" he muttered fiercely, stepping in. It *had* to be his, he sure as hell

110

needed it now! Money was way too tight, and his forced retirement was coming at him like a freight train.

'Come inside, Gordon...'

Wordlessly, he stepped over the threshold.

As soon as his foot landed in the basement, he let out a low moan of exquisite pleasure. It was a toe curling sweet delight, an ice cold beer on a sweltering day, and a soft bed after a hard day's work all rolled up into a single sensation. He stood for a moment shivering in the total bliss of it.

And right behind *that* was a sense of power unlike any he had ever had. All the punks in the prison he shoved around with impunity, the assholes he beat on when he was a kid, the small animals he tortured in secret— all of those moments of joyous power put together were nothing compared to what washed over him right now!

He brought his hands to his head to keep it from exploding. His feet faltered and he staggered. "Oh my God!" he muttered. "Oh my loving GOD!"

Yeeesssss...

He fell to his knees before this... this *presence*. When his knees rested on the bare floor the waves of pleasure and power swept over him again. "Oh my loving GOD!" he growled into the dirt. He stretched himself prone, arms and legs extended and felt the

111

pleasure intensify to the point of causing his vision to blur. Spikes of purple and red flashed in his brain.

It was beautiful.

"For you, my lord, for youuuu…" he moaned, his lips rubbing along the hard earth. He stuck his tongue out and licked the hard surface. "With you always… always with you…" he repeated it over and over, grinding his body into the dirt floor.

He went still when the sensations passed. He drew in a deep breath. He felt crumbs of dirt on his tongue and swallowed them all. Breathing heavily, he staggered to his feet and looked around.

The room was dark but for the moonlight coming though the basement entrance. Next time he'd bring a flashlight. And by all that's holy, there would be a next time. It was about time things started falling into place.

Above him, a floorboard creaked and was followed by low, thudding footsteps. His temple throbbed knowing that it was either the cabbie or his bitch. They were making themselves totally at home upstairs, in *his* house.

"Where are you?" he whispered softly.

The only thing he heard were voices and more floorboards creaking from above. His teeth ground. If he could get his hands on them, he'd kill them...eventually. First he'd wipe that smart ass look from the cabbie's face. He had a good idea how to do that. How would the cabbie feel watching his wife being beaten with a hammer? That would do the trick, all right.

'Yes, then the house will be yours.'

He spun around looking for the source of the soft murmur. The only visible thing was a thin strip of light at the top of a set of wooden steps. He took a step forward and stumbled when his foot thudded against something the wooden landing of the staircase. He lurched, flailing his arms like windmills as he fell towards the steps.

He gasped. His falling stopped in midair, held by an invisible something. It was cold... cold as steel as it pressed him back up onto his feet. His mouth gaped open and his head pivoted around. "Where are you?"

'Easy Gordon. You don't want them to see you...not yet.'

This time the voice was to his left. When his head jerked to see, the voice became a low chuckle. His heartbeat was fast and he panted, trying to see where it was. He'd heard enough to know it was a man.

'They have to be gone from here before the baby is born.'

113

Gordon's teeth ground together so hard one cracked and a piece broke off. He spat it onto the dirt packed floor and his gaze flew to the slice of light at the top of the stairs. A baby! Well wasn't that just a sweet little set-up—the young family settled in a new home. His fists clenched and un-clenched. There'd be neither family, nor baby in *his* house.

A shadow broke the line of light under the door at the top of the stairs. He heard a 'meeeooooow!' and a series of hisses, then claws scratching against it. He stepped back from the landing. It was that fucking cat he saw in the window!

'Leave now, but come back. There is a way...'

The voice in his head was followed by the sound of footsteps overhead. Gordon turned and slipped out the door, pulling it almost, but not completely shut, behind him. At the top of the steps he swept snow into the stairwell, covering his tracks. He retraced his steps walking backwards, swishing his feet to conceal his footprints. It was probably a waste of effort, they wouldn't be coming around to the back of the house. Why would they in the dead of winter?

He chuckled as he trudged through the snow and back onto the utility path. The dead of winter. Hah! He liked the sound of that.

114

<u>Chapter 12</u>

December 21, 2016, Winter Solstice

Myra got off the bus and trudged the fifty feet down the laneway to their home. It was a week since the incident in the spare room upstairs and things had been quiet. Even so, every time she entered the house, her gaze darted around, unsure of what would meet her.

She'd even gone back to saying prayers on a regular basis; not just every now and then. Nightly prayer had been a habit all through grade school and even the first few years of high school. But she stopped when she was in the eleventh grade; the stupid and tragic deaths of Mom and Dad turned her away from God.

The priest had tried to console Tony and her. He told them that Mom and Dad were in a far better place but she never bought into that. Her parents loved them. For them, nothing would have been better than being with their kids every day. Who did God think he was to destroy her family like that?

She started having second thoughts about that decision when this last pregnancy began. If anything, the earlier miscarriages taught her that life was a miracle.

In the foyer, she shrugged off her coat and hung it up. Looking to the living room, and then up the staircase, she shuddered. A quote from the Old Testament had been running through her head since that day of the 'visitation from Evelyn':

"There are yet hid greater things than these be, for we have seen but a few of his works."

She was still resentful of what God had done to her parents. But she hoped he was still in her corner. She had a strong feeling that she and Barry were going to need all the help they could get. She had even taken to wearing her gold crucifix again.

The cat slinked down the hall and began tracing figure eight patterns through her legs with its sleek body. She slipped her feet out of the winter boots and bent to pick Leia up. The cat immediately began purring and rubbing its head against her chin.

"How's my little Princess?" She scratched its ear and held it close, wandering through the dining room and then into the kitchen. Leia purred louder and its eyes blinked with lazy ease as she pushed her head into Myra's fingers for more.

When she went to put it down, it climbed higher on her shoulder and licked her ear lobe. Myra smiled and held the cat close, meandering into the kitchen. The cat never wanted to leave her when she was home. It tolerated Barry but it was obvious the cat adored her. The feeling was fast becoming mutual.

Gosh, she was bone tired. With only four days until Christmas, the stores were crazy busy. That in turn, spilled over into the food industry. She plugged in the kettle and took a mug from the cabinet to plop a tea bag into it. After topping up Leia's food dish and water, the cat hopped down. Myra yawned and trudged over to the table.

Her eyebrows drew together in a weary frown. Where was the book she'd been reading that morning? She was burning through Stella's old books and the one on spiritual cleansing rituals had really caught her attention. There was still an hour or so until Barry would be home and she'd been looking forward to just chillin' for a bit.

She bent to check under the table and then glanced at the wide window sill next to her normal seat. Nothing. A quick glance at the counter, the washer and dryer tucked in the corner also came up empty.

117

With her hands on her hips she paused. Where the hell was it?

She bumped the heel of her hand against her forehead at the next thought. Barry may have stopped at the house during the day and put it somewhere. She stepped into the library and looked around at the desk, chair and small table. She really hadn't expected to find it there since neither one of them particularly liked being in that room. She sighed and walked through the arch going into the living room. That room, like always, was cold and gave her the willies. It was probably her imagination, but every time she entered the room her chest felt heavy; taking a breath required a little bit more effort.

She gave the room a once over and huffed a sigh. Nada. But when she turned to cross back through to the front hallway she spied the corner of the book peeking out from under the chair beside the fireplace. Her eyes narrowed. What the hell is it doing there? Just as she touched it, there was a whoosh of air and the sudden flaming brightness of the fireplace starting up.

She yelped and sprang back up to her feet, clutching the book. Oh my God! For a moment, she froze with fear watching the yellow tongues above the blue gas flames in the grate. They reminded her of teeth.

Taking a deep breath, she reached to turn the knob that activated the jets of gas. But as quick as the flames had started, they stopped before her fingers even touched the brass knob. Her heart was going a mile a minute as she stared at the grate and the brickwork surrounding it. This was dangerous! The fireplace shouldn't be starting and stopping like that, all on its own.

The curtain at the side of the window billowed out catching her attention. It fluttered in the air, held aloft by some invisible hand. Myra stood riveted to the spot, barely breathing. Oh my God! Something was there. The curtain jerked up and down, like it was boldly taunting her.

She flinched at the rumbling growl and hiss next to her leg. Myra looked down to see the cat's back arched, every hair standing on end hissing at the curtain. Her paw spiked out, batting in the air before she raced across the room and through the front foyer.

Myra's knees trembled. She turned slightly and inch by inch, she backed away. Her gaze never wavered from the dangling curtain. When her foot thumped on the leg of the coffee table, she barely stopped herself from toppling over it, her feet moving fast to keep from falling.

She puffed air quickly, standing still and glaring at the curtain. After a few moments, she was able to control her breathing and her teeth clenched tight. Frig! If she'd fallen, she may have done some serious harm to the baby! Enough was enough.

Barry's words about this 'thing' feeding on fear flitted through her head. Her hand flew up to clasp the tiny crucifix hanging around her neck. "The Lord is my Shepherd. He maketh me to...."

Her eyebrows drew together, trying to remember the rest of that prayer. Shit! She could picture Sister Mary Arthur's plain face, her lips barely covering her horsey teeth as she recited it. She should have paid more attention to the words and not the teeth.

She took a deep breath, her voice booming, "The Lord protects me! He's on my side! Get out of my house, whatever you are!"

Her eyes opened wider when the curtain faltered, slipping down lower and lower. It was working! She made the sign of the cross over her head and shoulders, once more stepping back towards the entrance. "Please God..."

The curtain flopped down, waving slightly and coming to a complete standstill. Beside her, the cat let out one last growl before stalking off to the kitchen.

Myra let out a long sigh, closing her eyes. She hadn't even known she was holding her breath. Her legs were wobbly when she walked through the dining room. The smell of lilacs drifted in the air, and she felt calmer breathing it in. It had worked! Whatever had been in that room playing with the curtains hadn't liked her prayer nor the crucifix hanging around her neck.

She moved in a daze, still totally smoked by what had just happened. She unplugged the kettle and poured the water into her mug. She was about to use the spoon to stir and punch the flavor from the bag when she felt the baby.

Her eyes flashed wide and her hand jerked to her stomach to press gently. It was like someone was lightly scratching her, deep inside. She'd read about this and hadn't expected it for another couple of weeks.

It was the quickening—the baby moved deep inside her being. Tears burned the back of her eyes as she stood there in silent wonder. First contact from Isabella.

<u>Chapter 13</u>

Barry had traded vehicles with Alex that afternoon. Alex's taxi was a minivan and Barry needed one for this errand. He wheeled into his laneway, well aware of the extra two feet of scotch pine hanging out the back hatch. Myra had made a thing about a big Christmas tree when she'd first seen the place...he couldn't wait to see the look on her face when she saw this one!

He parked the vehicle and turned the headlights off. It was only five p.m. and already dark outside. Yeah. That made sense. It was December twenty-first, the longest night, the Winter Solstice.

He went to the back of the van and began to haul the great beast of a tree out of the tight space. A low light from the dining room window beamed on the snowy front yard, highlighting some of the newer flakes in a myriad of magical sparkles. Barry smiled. A white

Christmas, a tree and family coming over for Christmas dinner...what could be better?

After dragging the bushy evergreen across the driveway and up the step, he thrust the door open. Before entering, he swung the tree so that it rested on the base and bounced it a few times on the veranda to shed snow and loose needles there, rather than on the floor inside. When he stepped into the foyer, tugging the tree after him, he looked into the dining room. Where was she?

"Myra?" His voice boomed through the hallway and into the kitchen.

She appeared, still in the navy waitress uniform, the short sleeves trimmed in a white cuff over her slender arms, hands resting on her tummy, walking slowly towards him. There was something mysterious about the look on her face. She wore a smile under eyes that seemed to shimmer with happiness.

It came to him in a rush. She'd felt the baby move. But behind that thought another followed quickly. There had been a threat to her, from something in the room next to him. He propped the tree against the wall and stepped over to her. He looked into her eyes while his hand rose to settle on her belly.

Her eyes opened wider, "Oh! There it is again. Did you feel it?

123

It never registered in his palm but he felt it in his mind, the tiny foot stretching and pushing against her womb. Isabella. His chest was light as air, feeling like he'd float up to the ceiling and burst if it got any bigger. "Wow." He leaned down and kissed his wife, feeling the deep connection between the three of them.

Neither one of them noticed the cat slip out the front door that was still open. Neither one noticed the faint fragrance of lilac in air overpowered by the scent of the tree.

It was a lapse they'd regret later.

Chapter 14

Barry's gut clenched tight. The pizza he'd had sat like a lump of lead when he opened the spare bedroom door. The last time he'd been in that room had been spooky as hell and he and Myra had a terrible fight. So no good memories about going in there again.

But there was no choice. They needed the Christmas decorations that were stored in that room. He stepped inside and immediately the hair on his forearms spiked high and tingled.

The room was only partially furnished and it was Stella's stuff—an oak dresser with an antique pitted mirror mounted on hinges, and a single bed. Barry had stacked many cardboard boxes filled with seasonal items and other things they didn't need immediately, along the wall. His shoulders shuddered in the chilly air as he looked around for the box of decorations.

It was in the corner, the outside clearly labeled in Myra's handwriting. He strode over and picked it up from the floor, carrying it quickly in his arms past the bureau. An old woman's face, it's skin gnarled and twisted flitted on the mirror in the edge of his vision. He jerked to a stop and turned his head to look at it full on.

The only face that was there now was his own. His heart beat faster and his gaze flickered to the room behind him, reflected in the glass. The bed was to his left. He gasped seeing an area depress in the quilted comforter, like someone was sitting down on it. Whoever had been in the mirror before was now behind him, watching him from the centre of the bed! He could feel a disturbed rage emanate from that spot on the bed like a stench. How dare he enter her space.

He took a deep breath and turned around slowly, facing the bed. A shimmering outline of a woman faced him. This wasn't the same figure from the first time though. Whereas Evelyn was a delicate and ethereal, this being was coarse and earthy.

Where her eyes should be were two black holes, and her face was rife with scars from past diseases. Her hair hung in a loose, grey tangle far down past her shoulders. She grinned at him with blackened, stained teeth as a hand with cracked yellow nails reached out to him. A scent of rot infused the room.

Yup. Sure as shit, this wasn't Evelyn! He stepped back, the lower part of his back bumping into the edge of the bureau. The thought of her hand touching him filled him with dread. She shouldn't be there. She belonged in another dimension, one that he wanted no part of, not until it was his time. It wasn't natural that she would be there.

Anger rose like bile in the back of his throat. This was his home. Stella had left it to him and no ghost or spooky antics were going to drive him and Myra away. They weren't flesh and blood--they couldn't hurt him, only scare the crap out of him. He'd had enough of the pranks and scare tactics.

"You have no place in this world. Go back to wherever you came from." His voice was stronger and louder than he'd thought possible, considering how dry his mouth had become.

The hand rose higher, coming ominously close to his arm. But the face began to fade, the shimmering body becoming a misty vapor. The depression on the bed was no more. But a faint touch whispered along his neck and jaw, the icy chill of it making his blood run cold. The specter disappearing was a brief respite. This was its way of letting him know that.

The unnatural creepiness of the thing sank into his consciousness like a knife.

127

His jaw clenched and he strode out of the room, banging the door behind him.

"Barry? Is everything okay up there?" Myra's voice called from the stairwell. Before he had a chance to answer, she spoke again. "Is Leia up there? I can't find her."

He snorted, rounding the newel post and starting down the steps. "Nope. No Leia." Under his breath he muttered, "...just the normal, spooky shit."

The tree stood in the corner of the living room closest to the hallway. It wasn't ideal. They both would have preferred that it be in the dining room but that was out of the question with the family coming over for the big feast at Christmas. They'd need all the space they could get in that room.

He carried the box to the floor in front of the tree and set it down. "Maybe the cat's hiding. The humongous tree and the smell of it may have put her off. Cats don't like change in their space."

Myra folded her arms over her chest stepping into the room. "I'm glad it's in this corner of the room, far from the fireplace. You know, that thing started up all on its own earlier...and the curtain lifted."

Barry opened the box and tugged the set of lights out purposely not meeting her eyes. That was two things in the space of as many hours that something had happened. Whatever ghostly thing at work here, it was ratcheting things up.

If only Stella had provided more information on how to control this. How had she done it for so many years? And with the baby to worry about as well...he sighed. Looking over to Myra, he said, "The fireplace lit up all by itself?"

She nodded. "And then the curtain started flapping like a flag in a thunderstorm!"

"Holy shit."

Myra grinned. "Well, holy something or another. I said a prayer and it stopped."

When he looked over at her, her cheeks were flushed pink and there was a shy smile on her lips.

She rolled her eyes and continued, walking closer to him and helping sort the tangle of brightly colored lights. "Well, not a real church type prayer...more like, 'God's on my side, so git!' type thing, but whatever...it worked."

He paused and couldn't help the wide grin that spread on his face watching her. Myra was really something else! She was probably scared to death but she'd dealt with it. She'd even had her first mother daughter experience afterwards.

He winked and flashed a grin at her. "I especially like the 'git'. Very celestial of you."

She landed a punch on his arm but a soft giggle followed. "Yeah. It sounds hokey but whatever works, right?" She tossed the lights at his feet and started towards the back of the house. "I'm worried about the cat. She's always at my feet and I don't think she's hiding because of the tree."

He plugged the lights into the wall socket and began to string them on the branches. In the kitchen he could hear her calling for the cat and shaking the box of kibble. That and the sound of the fridge opening usually brought Leia on the run.

His jaw tightened. If it didn't show up by the time they went to bed, he'd check that spare room in case it slipped in there when he went to get the lights. It was probably a good idea anyway, to make sure things were quiet. If not, he'd just tell it to 'git.' He shook his head and smiled.

****

A couple hours later, the cat was still missing and Myra was almost in tears. "What if it got out when you brought the tree in? The door was open for a while." They were on their way up the stairs for the night but she double backed and unlocked the front door.

A whoosh of cold air poured in the front doorway when she stood there calling, "Leia! Here kitty, kitty."

Barry went back down the few steps and joined her at the door, putting his arm over her shoulder, "Look, the cat first showed up from down in the cellar. Maybe it found a way in and it's down there again." He shook his head and sighed. "I should have thought of that earlier."

He closed the door and nudged her towards the stairs. "You go up to bed. I'll check the cellar."

She smiled feebly and then turned, taking the stairs slowly. He could tell by her body language that she despaired of him ever finding Leia. Actually, he didn't have a good feeling about it either but he had to try, at least go through the motions. The cat could have run to the street and been hit by a car for all he knew. But he'd check the cellar...just in case.

There was a flashlight on the counter in the kitchen that he grabbed before walking over to the cellar door. He didn't trust that place. It had a bad feeling about it and the lights were as likely to go off all by themselves as not. He opened the door and flicked the light switch, lighting the centre of the cellar and the rickety old stairs.

His chest fell when he stepped forward. If the cat was down there, it should have raced by him to get to its food in the kitchen, now that the door was open. But the only movement was the light bulb swaying slightly, hanging from the low ceiling. His grip on the flashlight tightened when he stepped down onto the packed dirt floor.

The furnace was a hulking monster taking up one section of the room. The flames flickered in the small crease around the firebox and there was a low thrum of its motor. The smell of heating oil and mold filled Barry's nostrils.

"Here kitty. Are you in here, Leia?" His voice was barely above a whisper, looking around the room for the sight of anything light in color. When he stepped closer to the centre of the room a cobweb coated his cheek. His hand rose to swipe it away. Shit. The place smelled and felt horrible.

The bowels of the earth where evil churned. He shuddered. Now why had that thought popped into his head? It was all bad enough down there without his inner voice adding fuel to the fire.

He took a deep breath and pulled his shoulders higher, walking slowly to the far wall. There was a flicker of the light bulb and then everything went black. He gasped and jerked back for a moment.

After taking a deep breath, his fingers fumbled with the button on the flashlight and a beam of light lit the far wall. Even though he'd been prepared for something weird to happen with the light in the cellar, when it happened, it still made his heart hammer in his chest.

He swung his hand, aiming the light in all the dark recesses of the room. Nothing. He'd known that cat wasn't here but—

Above him, there was a crash and the sound of glass breaking. His eyes almost popped out onto his cheeks as he stared at the ceiling, heard another set of thumps. His heart now thudding like a jackhammer, he scrambled back to the stairs, taking them two at a time. The door at the top was closed. He hadn't heard it swing shut and for sure *he* hadn't closed it!

At first the handle wouldn't budge when he tried turning it. He gripped it tighter, pulling it towards his body, trying hard to get it to turn. What the hell was up there banging around? What about Myra? He knew she hadn't made the noise. A feeling of dread filled him.

The door latch made a loud click and immediately it swung open. Again, it happened on its own, even though he'd been giving it his all. A chill of foreboding skittered up his spine when he stepped out of the basement. The noise had sounded like it was coming from the living room.

He hurried down the hall and stopped short in the archway. Oh my God! It was impossible!

He blinked a few times and his jaw fell open. The Christmas tree was upside down! It balanced on a few thin branches pressing the floor and the thicker part of the trunk was only inches from the ceiling!

What felt like a bead of ice trickled down his spine. How the hell was the tree standing like that? Shit! He'd only been downstairs a few minutes! What the hell kind of entity was in this house? His heart raced and his legs felt weak, like he could collapse at any minute.

Myra's footsteps sounded on the stairs behind him and he turned to face her, shaking his head in disbelief.

Looking past him to the evergreen, her eyes were round with fright and her fingers like talons dug into his arm. "Oh sweet Jesus!"

'*A cheap parlor trick. Don't be afraid.*' Stella's voice was soothing, a whisper in his mind.

With a crackling thud, the tree tumbled to the floor. Branches snapped and ornaments smashed under the impact. Both Barry and Myra jolted a step backwards.

Her head turned slowly and her face was blanched of all color, lips gaping wide. "Barry, I'm scared." She stepped closer and clung to him. Her eyes were once more on the bushy spruce tree laying in the midst of silver tinsel and spun glass shards. She was stiff and shivering against him.

He was having a hard time holding himself up, let alone being strong for Myra but he had to. Whatever had flipped the tree upside down and then let it fall was gone. He could feel it deep inside, like a weight had lifted from his body.

He took a deep breath, tightening his grip on his wife as he pulled his chest and shoulders up. The scent of lilacs was sudden, overpowering the smell of the tree. His mouth set in a grim line staring at the downed tree. Stella had been right. It was a cheap parlor trick, quite literally *in* the parlour.

"Guess the resident ghost doesn't like the tree. Do you suppose it was the angel on the top? Maybe he, she, it...prefers a star." He snorted and kissed the top of Myra's head. If they couldn't scrape up a laugh over this, they'd cry, that was for sure.

"Did you say she it? Because I'm inclined to agree with you. The ghost is a total shit—not he or she." She looked up at him and her face was more relaxed.

"Absolutely! I can't think of a better name." He looked over at the tree and his voice was loud when he spoke. "Hey Shit! You made quite a mess with our tree! It was our first real Christmas tree too. Thanks a lot, Shithead!"

135

He began to laugh, pulling Myra along with him when he turned and walked down the hall to the kitchen. He could understand how dark humor helped surgeons, and soldiers cope. The tree balancing on its tip was impossible, except that they'd both seen it. What they were dealing with was really going all out to freak them out.

Myra paused and called over her shoulder to the living room. "Just for that, I'm buying more *angel* decorations and putting them all over the tree. Angels, the Crèche...anything religious, just to piss you off, Shit."

Barry chuckled and felt a little more at ease...not completely there, but better now that Myra was also sharing the humor. "I'll make you some chamomile tea, Babe. I'm having something stronger."

She laughed and her hand drifted over her tummy. "I could use a stiff drink too, but I'll settle for the tea."

When they entered the kitchen, there was an envelope centered on the bare table. It was battered and torn near the one side and looked like it was ancient.

Myra stepped away from him and picked it up. "What's this?" She flipped the cover back and pulled a document from inside. Her eyes flashed to meet Barry's puzzled look.

"It's some sort of record...it's hard to tell because it's really old and it's handwritten." Myra looked over at him. "It wasn't here earlier. Do you think it could be Stella's?"

Chapter 15

Myra flopped into the chair and laid the paper on the table in front of her. Her knees were rubbery from what she'd just seen in the living room. How the hell had the Christmas tree flipped and then balanced on its tip? What kind of force was in the house that could *do* that?

And now, finding the envelope laying there, completely out of the blue...what else could happen that night? *Strange* was becoming the new normal. Still...she huffed a long sigh through pursed lips.

Barry cracked a beer and chugged half of it walking over to join her at the table. He pulled a chair close to hers and leaned close to read what was written on the page. The handwriting was spidery, but legible.

May 16 1992

Regarding the junction of the Frontenac and the Forty-fourth ley lines:

Concession 4,Parcel 6, Farm Lot 15, is the junction of these two magnetic ley lines, a source of immense supernatural and paranormal power.

Once, it was a sacred meeting place for Native people, but the land became property of the Crown and was deeded for farm use to early colonial settlers. In the mid eighteen hundreds or thereabouts, the current residential home was constructed.

The earliest known record of paranormal activity was made by Evelyn Braithwaite, my aunt, a spinster who lived at the property and died in her eighty-eighth year. According to her testimony, malevolent forces or spirits linger at this juncture. When left unguarded, these powers escape their dimension to wreak havoc among mankind.

There are a number of these powerfully charged junctions across the earth and at critical times throughout history, security has been breached with disastrous results. Shots fired at Fort Sumter in Charleston Bay in April 1861 were the start of the American Civil War. In January 1933 Hitler rose to power. Rwanda April

139

1994. Jim Jones November 1978 who led almost one thousand people to commit suicide.

These are but a small sampling of the breaches of the junctures. Human history is rife with examples.

For this reason, it is imperative that — shaman, white witch, psychic or clairvoyant— whatever name is ascribed to such a person, that he or she assume stewardship of these sites.

In the case of 26 Centre Street, I, Stella Braithwaite, inherited the responsibility of stewardship, from my Aunt, Evelyn Braithwaite. While it is preferable that the task of suppressing entry of malevolent, evil spirits, be transferred to a blood heir, it is not advisable in my case.

With neither direct descendent and the only other heir found to be entirely unsuitable for this responsibility, it is with some reluctance and trepidation that I am forced to seek a stranger— a benevolent and gifted person willing to assume the mantle of responsibility.

Myra looked over at her husband. "That's you, Barry. You were the person she found to look after this house." She turned back to the document and flipped it over, looking for anything more, any footnote. "She left this here for us to find."

"Which is kind of weird...why wouldn't she have included it with the legal papers in the lawyer's office?"

"I think I know." Myra tapped the papers. "Include this in the will and testament and you have a strong case for *not* being of sound mind and body." She looked up at Barry. "It might have given that Gord creep ammunition to have the will voided."

"You got a point," Barry sighed and got up to unplug the kettle and make her tea. "I'm still not sure what it is that I'm supposed to do..." His hands rose and he pantomimed quotation marks with his fingers, "... in order to *guard* this spot. Seems to me I'm not doing such a bang up job when Shithead in there, wrecked our tree."

Myra's forehead tightened in thought looking at the document once more. "Barry. It seems to me that Stella's leading you with this, just a bit at a time." She picked up the letter and her hand jerked. "This. It appears right after we get the shock of our lives, seeing that tree." She shuddered. "That still freaks me out."

"I know, me too. Stella was here. I sensed her. And now finding the letter, just confirms it." He picked up the mug of steaming liquid and walked over to the

141

table, taking a seat next to her again. "Every time one of these weird things happen, I hear her in my head. She tells me not to be afraid."

Myra held the mug in both hands, blowing softly on the surface to cool it. "Easier said than done, of course. And the cat is still missing." She didn't need any psychic ability to know that its disappearance and the tree episode were related.

"Today's the winter solstice, you know. It's also the worst day we've had yet in terms of paranormal stuff happening." Barry's mouth pulled to the side and he rolled his eyes. "No coincidence, I'm sure." He picked up the letter and a small smile curled his lips gazing at it. "Yeah. Stella *chose* this day to show this letter to us. I can feel her right now."

Myra jerked at the sensation deep inside. Her hand fell to her stomach and a well of happiness filled her chest. Isabella. She reached for Barry's hand and placed it on her tummy. "Stella's namesake is also sensing something."

<u>Chapter 16</u>

The sounds of banging downstairs woke Myra from a sound sleep. She reached for Barry only to find his side of the bed empty and cool. With arms stretched above her head, she glanced over at the window, and smiled seeing the golden rays of the sun shine through.

As the events of the night before came to mind, her hands fell to the bedspread with a thud. Barry was probably cleaning up the mess in the living room and setting the tree up again. She threw the covers back and got out of bed, already sliding her feet into her slippers and slipping her robe on. The cat. She had to see if it had come back.

When she was at the last few steps at the bottom, Barry stepped out of the living room, watching her. He shook his head softly in answer to the silent question in her eyes. Leia was still missing.

"I got the tree back up! This time, I nailed the tree stand to the floor and screwed the tree into it. It's

143

not going anywhere now. Surprisingly, not every ornament broke. Shithead missed a few." He stepped over and gave her a quick kiss. "How about after breakfast we go out shopping together? You're off and I can go in late. I think we both need a break from this place after last night."

She glanced past him into the living room where the lower branches of the tree could be seen through the archway. The floor was swept clean. It was hard to believe what had happened the night before was real and not a dream. But it had happened, along with another visit from Stella.

"Sure. Sounds great." She tried to sound upbeat but the cat was still a worry in the back of her mind. She walked over to the door and opened it. The front step was empty and there was no sign of it in the laneway.

At the sound farther down the front of the house, she turned to look. A couple crows were on the ground, their wings flapping as they pecked at each other in a fight for something on the ground between them. When the one nearest moved to the side, a flash of red in the snow and a lump next to it appeared.

Her heart sank like a stone and she turned to thrust her feet into her winter boots.

"Myra? What the—"

"It's Leia. I've got to see." She sprinted out the front door waving her arms to scare the crows away. The blood streaked fur and body of the cat lay in a mangled heap in the snow under the living room window.

Tears filled Myra's eyes and she lowered to her knees in the snow. The cat looked like its neck was broken, its body frozen solid and the eyes open. Poor little Leia. The cat had been her first pet. The sweet little thing had really liked her. She wiped a tear from her cheek. It didn't deserve what had happened to it. It was the house. Somehow, it was responsible for Leia's death.

At Barry's footsteps, she turned and watched him squat next to her. His face was tight and his brown eyes sad, watching her. "I'm sorry, Myra. Why don't you go inside? I'll take care of Leia."

She rose and with leaden feet, trudged slowly back to the entrance. When she was inside, she leaned against the door and closed her eyes, the tears rolling down her cheeks. The cat had always followed her around the house. It had really bonded with her and she with it. The poor little thing...it wasn't fair what had happened to it.

So far, whatever spooky shit had happened in the house hadn't hurt anyone. But now the stakes had risen higher. She swiped the tears from her cheeks and sniffed loudly. The winter boots bounced off the wall when she kicked them off.

She stomped into the living room. Her teeth ground together and she balled her hands into fists at her sides, glaring around the room. Of course, she couldn't see anything out of order, but she knew it was there. She could almost hear the soft laughter in the walls.

"Okay Shithead, this is war. You should never have killed my cat."

The fireplace ignited with a hiss and then dancing flames appeared. Beside her, the Christmas tree branches quivered and the tree top bent side to side. Myra jerked back for a moment but then her eyes became narrow slits of rage. The ghost or spirit or whatever the hell was dominating this part of the house was mocking her!

Well two could play at that game. She'd get the last word but not until later. First she had to get a handle on all of this paranormal crap. There had to be a way of fighting this thing. Myra had been an 'A' student in school. It was now time to do some serious research.

She glanced at Stella's upholstered chair as she turned to leave the room. How the hell had the old lady managed to live there for so long keeping a lid on this horrible energy?

****

Gordon had also woken up. He had a hangover. When he shuffled into the bathroom, he was glad he wore gloves last night. That stupid cat only managed to nick him a little bit before he snapped its damn neck.

He bobbed his eyebrows in the mirror and smiled.

"One down, two to go."

<u>Chapter 17</u>

Barry went to the trunk of the cab and got the heavy plastic shopping bag. Today, he wouldn't be needing it to pick up odd items at the grocery store. Today, it would serve as Leia's burial shroud. He sighed and his feet crunched the hard packed snow walking back to the house to get the cat. He felt bad bundling the cat up so unceremoniously but hell, what could he do? If the ground wasn't frozen, he would have buried it next to the pond in the back yard.

Myra was so upset there was no way he'd go into details of how he'd dispose of the cat's body. It was stiff as a board when he slipped it into the bag. He walked back to the cab and set it in the trunk, closing the lid softly afterwards.

When he got back inside the house, Myra was in the kitchen making breakfast. She stood at the counter, with her back to him when he entered. He walked over and put his arms around her, pulling her gently into his body. "Are you okay, sweetie?"

She turned and he could tell by the set of her jaw, her chin held high that she was pissed. His eyes met hers and a wave of relief flooded through his gut. Anger was better than feeling the sorrow of the cat's death, right? Watching her cry would have torn his heart out.

"Okay? Hardly! But I will be." Her hands drifted up from his waist to the middle of his back and he could feel her fingertips press firmly. "We need to know more about what we're dealing with, Barry." She sighed. "I really wish that Stella had enlightened you. Maybe if she'd told you that she was leaving the house to you, and what was here, we'd be in a better position to deal with it."

The day the old lady died flashed in his mind. She had known her time was close; why hadn't she said anything? Had she worried that if he'd really known the true situation, he would have said no? The cat being killed left a queasy feeling in his gut. The next time, would it be one of them or something that would threaten the baby? The stakes were getting dangerously high.

"Maybe you were right when you said we should go back to the apartment. We were happy before and at least we were safe back then." He looked down

149

at the floor for a moment. "Whatever is in this house really wants us gone. The tree last night, the cat..."

"Barry? You know what's wrong with you? You're not a fighter. You'd rather get along with people, even get stiffed sometimes on your fares rather than get into a hassle. Don't get me wrong. I love that you're a pacifist but there comes a time when you have to draw a line in the sand."

His mouth fell open watching her. He *was* trying to keep his family safe! Stella had been wrong in choosing him for this task. It would take a person with more power than he had...fuck!

He didn't even *want* this psychic ability shit. It had cost him his mother and he wasn't about to let it cost him Myra and the baby!

"Myra! It's not worth the risk to me! If something happened..."

Her lip quivered for a moment before she looked into his eyes again. "No Barry. Leia was my line in the sand. Killing a helpless animal? No way am I sitting back and taking that!"

Her hands fisted the front of his shirt. "We're not running away. We're making progress here because *it* or whatever the hell it is, is fighting harder. God only knows what we've done but whatever it is, we've pissed it off."

She huffed a fast sigh through flared nostrils. "Well, I'm pissed as well. I'm going to spend the day getting more information on this ley line and supernatural stuff. Knowledge is power too." She pointed in the direction of the office Barry had set up. "Stella left us a ton of books about this—maybe that's all we need. *I'm* going to read up on this stuff too." She held up her finger. "Starting today."

Barry knew there was no talking her out of this. When Myra made up her mind, she could be stubborn.

'Accept this part of yourself, Barry. You may need to use it sometime.' Stella's words in the cab that day sounded in his mind. Stella had chosen him. She had confidence in him and now here was Myra, essentially saying the same thing.

The psychic gift wasn't something he'd ever wanted but he was stuck with it. Instead of fighting that fact, he needed to join Myra in fighting the evil in the house. Stella had known it was important and deep down, he knew it too.

****

It was after seven when he drove the cab into the laneway at their house. Myra had called earlier in the afternoon to let him know she was catching the bus home. She knew how busy he was the few days before Christmas ferrying last minute shoppers to and from the mall. Considering how the day had started out, she had sounded pretty upbeat.

Still, it was a surprise to see every light in the house blazing from the windows out onto the snow covered yard. He parked the car and walked into the house. What was she up to?

A pungent smell, like grass smoldering filled his nostrils, while ahead of him on the stairs, a chunky white candle burned.

"Myra?" He hung his coat on the hook and stepped from the foyer, peeking into the living room. The tree was still upright and she'd hung angel decorations all over it. The small crèche they'd bought was set up near the fireplace.

Even though neither of them went to church, they'd both been raised Christian, so the nativity scene meant something to them. Seeing the religious ornaments and the lingering scent in the air filled him with a sense of peace.

"Hi! How was your day?" She came up behind him holding a smoldering bundle of what looked like brown straw in her outstretched hand.

"I think the question is, how was *your* day? What's this?" He nodded to the straw, watching her raise it over his head and use it like an airport wand scanner along his body. He smiled at the intent look on her face, concentrating on what she was doing.

152

"Breathe it in. It's a sage and cedar smudge. It's supposed to purify. I've done the house and now I'm doing you. Same with the white candle and holy water." She finished her scan and leaned in to kiss his lips lightly.

"So this will get rid of Shithead or at least keep him out of this part of the house?" The cellar was something else altogether. It wasn't like they went down there very much anyway.

She shook her head. "We're not supposed to communicate with it. It's okay to command it to leave, but that's all we get to say to it." Her eyes narrowed watching him. "Can you feel it? I mean, I've been through the upstairs and down here with the smudge, holy water and candle. It feels better to me, but I'm not the sensitive psychic one here."

Myra hadn't mentioned going down to the basement, thank goodness. The very last place he ever wanted her to go, alone, was in that creepy hole. No. He'd find out what she'd done up in the main part of the house and replicate it in the cellar, all on his own.

After taking a deep breath and walking around the living room slowly, he turned to face her. "Actually, I think it feels lighter. I always felt depressed and had a harder time catching my breath in here. The air was kind of thick and soupy. It's better now."

153

"Well I really gave it a triple whammy in here and in the two rooms upstairs." She grinned and reached for his hand. "C'mon. I made some tea and there's lasagna in the oven."

"From John's Deli?" he asked.

"Where else?" She had introduced him to the joys of the pasta dishes from that store the first year they started going out. He had stopped trying to improve on the perfection of that dish.

He let her lead him through the hallway and into the kitchen. All the while he was looking around and opening his senses to anything weird. It was the first time he'd felt that they were alone, nothing watching them.

"I went through all the books Stella left us looking for information about these ley lines."

"Oh yeah? Find out anything new?"

"Well, the first thing, is that what you had inferred from that book you read is absolutely correct. The correlation between the events you talked about, and the one's Stella mentioned in her document— those events and 'disruptions of the lines' are pretty closely tied together."

"So there's more than the ones she had drawn on the globe?"

"Yeah. LOTS more. These electromagnetic ley lines connect energy hot spots in the earth's surface. You can think of the energy hot spots as 'chakras' of the earth, kind of like the chakras of the body that Eastern mysticism talks about." "It's a little strange, but if you think of the planet as a... a *person,* a being in its own right, this stuff makes sense." She watched him take a seat at the table.

"Oh yeah, I've heard of that perspective—the Gaia Hypothesis." He waved a hand in the air. "When I read it, it sounded too 'New Agey' for my taste." He put his hand on top of the table. "But now... I ain't so sure, doll."

Stella snorted. "If the government can tell us the General Motors is a person, why can't the Earth be one?"

"A person? You're saying the Earth has a personality?"

"Shhh. Don't get *too* into it. If that's the case, it doesn't mean we have the ability to understand it." She shrugged. "You know... we wouldn't expect an ant to understand *us* right? So how could we understand Mother Earth?"

Barry looked around the room. "Uh oh. Sage and sweetgrass. Candles and holy water." He grinned at her. "You're turning into a hippie!"

"I could care less. Whatever it takes to beat Shithead." Tears filled her eyes. "It's weird, Barry; but I really loved Leia. Coming home from work, knowing she was here... it made my day... I don't know... *fuller*." She looked away. "I didn't understand that connection people had with their pets 'till now."

He took her hand in his. "Hey... Something popped into my head. Maybe that's the way ol' Mother Earth feels towards us?"

She snickered. "Now who's the hippie?"

"Shit. Oh well, let's tie dye some tee shirts."

Even though the living room had felt cleaner, it would have been wishful thinking to suppose that everything was gone. There was still the cellar to deal with. But watching Myra, it was hard not to get caught up in the boost of her positive energy.

Before Barry looked down at the book she'd left open on the table, his peripheral vision had caught a few small sparks surrounding her head, floating in a wave of gold. The peace and happiness that she'd worked hard to bring to the house that day had infused her soul as well.

"Whoa..." he said softly.

"What?"

"You ain't gonna believe this, hon... but I'm starting to see auras now." He turned his head from her.

"Just out of the corner of my eye, I can see yours… it's really pretty."

They sat silently for a moment.

"I'm envious, Barry," she said with a smile. After another moment, she continued on with her status report. "I've poured lines of sea salt on all the doorways upstairs and on this level. It's supposed to cleanse the area. Entities despise being near it." Standing up, Myra slipped padded mitts on and opened the oven door to take the lasagna out and place it on top of the stove.

Barry grinned feeling wonder, watching the matter of fact way she was handling all of this. It was like she was outlining a regimen of spring cleaning, instead of ridding them of the forces that had killed the cat. "I'm glad you left the basement and attic till I came home. I'll do those rooms."

She spun around and placed her hands on her hips, instructing him. "It's important that you are calm and don't feel any fear. These things feed on our fear and become more powerful. And you need to invoke a higher power too."

"Wow! You've really been busy reading up on this stuff. You've got the ritual part down pat. Holy water, candles, salt and burning sage." His eyebrows lifted and he exhaled slowly. "I'm not sure about the religion stuff, but I'll do the rest."

She walked over to him and put her hand on his shoulder, looking down into his eyes. "We'll do it together. We both know that the north side of the house is the most affected by whatever is trying to sneak out. The ley line is the most concentrated there."

She shook her head and leaned closer, lowering her voice to a whisper. "It's evil, Barry. Stella's note said as much, and from what I read today, we need the help of a higher power, be it God, Jesus, the Creator, Jiminy Cricket or whatever. A power of goodness and light to combat the dark."

A shudder skittered down his spine as her words drifted into his ear. She was right but there was no way he wanted to endanger her or the baby. He sighed, already not liking what he was about to say. "What about getting a priest in to help me? I don't want you to get more involved. You've already done enough. Maybe a blessing..."

Myra smiled and put both hands on his shoulder, looking into his eyes. "I'm way ahead of you, Barry. Sometimes I think I'm the one with the ESP. I knew you wouldn't want me to help. So I went to Saint Mary's and spoke with a priest."

"Oh really?"

"Yes. And in fact, he says he knows you. Do you remember Philip Walsh?"

Of course he remembered Philip Walsh. He was one of the kids who was involved with that beating he had gotten as a kid. "Yeah, I know him."

Before he had a chance to answer she spoke again. "He's changed a lot since high school. He's a priest now and he'll be coming over to bless the house. He's just been assigned to Kingston."

Barry felt the muscles of his neck tighten but he held his tongue. Getting a priest in wasn't much of a stretch, if you think about it. But Philip Walsh?

Chapter 18

While Myra and Barry ate lasagna, Gordon Braithwaite was drinking his dinner. As usual he sat by his kitchen window.

The snow continued to fall; snowflakes streaked through the light cast from Gordon's window and then escaped into the blackness of the night. But Gordon neither saw nor cared about the storm outside.

He got up from his chair and staggered across the worn carpet and down the hall to the bathroom door. He braced his hands on the walls on each side to keep from falling, leaving fresh sweaty smudges on the already stained paint.

He finished his business and looked in the mirror while he washed his hands. Narrow, angry grey eyes stared back at him above a roadmap of broken veins in his pasty cheeks. All afternoon the rum and coke he'd been drinking acted like lighter fluid stoking the raw ember of anger brighter and brighter. A rumbling plume of alcohol belched out of loose lips before he turned away and stumbled back to his perch near the window.

It was almost a month since the funeral and he was still stuck in the scuzzy townhouse, while the cabbie and his bitch lived in the grand home that should have been his. Blood's thicker than water, and blood will always tell, right?

He *tried* to do it legit! After the funeral he saw two lawyers, the ones that advertised first consult as free. In both cases the shysters shook their heads slowly after he finished telling how his *only blood relative on Earth* had left him just a single dollar. And in both cases they told him he had no case. The will was solid.

He couldn't make them understand! Stella's will had been bogus! The cabbie had conned her into making him the heir. He knew enough inmates who'd tried going straight and had driven a cab to make money. They were crooks, every last one of them.

'Yes. They tricked her, Gordon. Now they're laughing at you, living it up in the old house. They'll get everything Gordo if you're not careful.'

His head jerked back and he looked around. Ever since he'd visited the house and broke into the cellar, voices whispered in his head. Not that he disagreed with the message...but Christ, they could happen right out of the blue and startle him so bad, he'd almost spilled his drink more than once.

And now the voice was taking on its own character. A deep, sonorous baritone, with just a touch of a British accent. Not the foppy plum in the mouth one; no… more like an older version of James Bond. When that voice spoke, he listened.

And replied.

"Yeah! I need to challenge that will. Take the bastards to court." His teeth ground together before he belted back the rest of the drink. "I can't challenge the will, so I'll just sue them!"

'That won't work. There are other ways. Think Gordo! You're smarter than them aren't you?' It chuckled deeply. *'After all, they're just a dumb cabbie and a waitress!'*

Gordon's fist tightened on the glass, forcing a hairline crack to appear. He rose and lurched across the room to the kitchen. After tossing the glass into the trash, he poured more rum into another one from the cabinet.

There had to be a way! Threaten them? Scare them? Bribery was out; he had no money. He wandered back to the window and sat down once more.

'The weak link. Look for their weakest point and strike hard.'

162

He nodded at the sage wisdom that whispered in his mind. The woman. She was the weak link...

His eyes widened and he sat back in the chair. She was pregnant. He'd be getting two for the price of one if he could threaten her life. That cabbie would sign over the deed to the house pretty fast if his wife's life was at stake.

'Kill them. Make it look like a murder suicide.'

Gordon chuckled and took a long swallow of his drink. Yeah. He'd make it look like the bastard was overcome with guilt that he'd played Stella and got everything from her. He'd relented and done the right thing, signed everything over to the rightful heir, Gordon. Immediately after, he killed his wife and then himself. It would all fall into place for the cops when they found the will and the deed signed over.

It was just a matter of choosing the right time.

Just as his days of living in a dumpy townhouse, working with lowlife scum were numbered...so were those of the cabbie and his wife.

Chapter 19

At 1:00 pm the following day Barry pulled into the wide driveway of his home. A black sedan was already parked there with the engine running. He parked behind it and got out. He closed the door and folded his arms across his chest. This was as far as he was willing to go until Phil said some things.

The driver's side door opened and he watched a man in a black overcoat step out and turn around.

He hadn't seen Phil since that afternoon when his nose got broken. Mom pulled him out of St. Mary's the next day and registered him at a public school. And now Phil Walsh was all grown up. The guy was Barry's age and had really packed on the pounds, the only reason he could still be called 'stout' was that he hadn't hit forty yet. Even under his coat, you could tell he was going to flab.

The two men stared at each other for a silent moment until Phil ran his hand through his thinning brown hair and trudged through the snow to Barry with his hand outstretched.

"It's been a long time, Barry," he said.

Barry looked down at the hand and back up. "We don't need to do that, Phil. My wife asked you here, not me. Let's get on with it, okay?"

"Hey..."

"The last time I saw *that* hand, it was coming at my face to do this," Barry laid a finger by the crook in his nose. He scoffed. "And now you're a priest..." he shook his head slowly. "Who woulda thunk it?"

"Barry... we were *children*. It was years and years ago." He drew a breath. "Children do and say things that as adults we'd never tolerate. They need to be taught, Barry, and then they need to be forgiven."

Phil's voice took on a timbre of someone addressing a crowd; his words placed carefully with a rhythmic pacing. He wasn't talking, the guy was preaching.

Philip looked down at the ground for a moment. "I can't change the past but I do regret what I did to you." He took a deep breath and glanced over at the house.

165

It was as much of an apology as Barry was likely going to get. He still didn't trust or like the guy but this wasn't about Barry. It was about Myra and the baby, keeping everyone safe, going through this ritual. He huffed a sigh and led the way over to the steps.

As they climbed to the veranda and Barry unlocked the door, Phil said, "Myra said you need the house blessed. She seemed pretty upset, rambling on about evil spirits." He looked sharply at Barry. "A house blessing is pretty common but the church's position on demons and entities..." Philip blew out a rush of air through pursed lips. "...let's just say that we, the church I mean...we maintain a healthy skepticism on that. This isn't the middle ages. *The Exorcist* was a sensationalist movie and that's all it was."

Barry turned to Philip after un-locking the front door with a sardonic smile. He was going to enjoy watching this phony, condescending prig experience the house. For the first time he was actually rooting for the spirit or ghost or whatever it was.

He extended his arm ushering the priest in. Philip slipped by him and stood in the foyer gazing up at the stairs and through the archways leading to the living and dining rooms.

"Nice house, Barry." There was a puzzled look in the priest's grey eyes. "You and Myra have done pretty well for yourselves, haven't you?" He cast a few glances over at Barry as he removed his boots and coat. "The service industry is more lucrative than I ever would have thought." It was a low mutter as he picked up the small case he'd carried in.

Barry decided to ignore the innuendo. There was no need to explain anything to an ass like Philip. It was none of his business how they'd come to live there. Once the blessing was complete, he'd never see Philip again and that was all there was to it.

Maybe if it hadn't been Philip...if Myra had gotten another priest, an older guy, he'd take this more seriously. But Philip? He could still see him in the gang of boys, taunting and throwing punches. "Should we start upstairs or the basement?" was all the reply he made.

BANG! The noise came from the second floor, and the area where they were standing suddenly became icy cold.

When Philip's head jerked back and he looked at the ceiling above him, Barry couldn't help but feel smug, waiting for the other man to look over at him. The air had gotten so cold that wisps of vapor formed in front of his face from his breath.

The sanctimonious, superior look in Philips' eyes was replaced with wide eyes darting to the staircase. "Is Myra—"

MICHELLE DOREY

"Nope. It's just us and something that you, and the church of course...that you say doesn't exist. I think we're supposed to start upstairs." The corners of Barry's lips twitched and he worked hard at keeping the grin off his face.

"That's not how it's done, Barry." Phil set his bag down in the foyer and opened it. He took out a prayer book and a silver flask the size of a pint.

"Don't tell me you're going to have a drink, man."

Phil gave a quick disgusted snort. Holding the bottle up, he said, "This is Holy Water, Barry." He opened the book to a flagged page. "We start at the entrance and work our way around the house to the upstairs."

Barry huffed a sigh as Phil pulled the cap from the bottle and sprinkled drops about the entrance.

Reading from the text, Phil said, "O God, protect our going out and our coming in; Let us share the hospitality of this home with all who visit us, that those who enter here may know your love and peace. Grant this through Christ our Lord." He looked over to Barry. "Here's the part where you're supposed to say 'Amen', remember?"

BANG!

Both men jumped.

Phil looked at Barry and bared his teeth. With flinty eyes, he said, "This isn't a funny joke, Barry. You're holding a grudge way too long."

Barry let out a huff. "You idiot. It's *not* me! I think we're being challenged, 'Father Phil'. You man enough to take it?"

BANG! BANG! BANG!

Phil rolled his eyes. "Oh for Heaven's sake! Fine! Let's get your stupid prank over with, okay?" He brushed past Barry and lumbered up the stairs. The banging from the bedroom increased in ferocity as he drew closer. At the top of the stairs, her turned and looked down his nose at Barry. "This is such *bullshit*. You're making light of my faith you asshole," he fumed.

"Wait up, Phil!" Barry called. He ran up the stairs to see Phil go down the hallway to the room where Evelyn and whatever foul spirit within had squared off as their battleground. From the racket, it was obvious that Evelyn was outgunned on this one. How had that happened?

Phil got to the door and the banging was now replaced by the doorknob rattling on its own. He stood in front of it, his lips curling in scorn. As Barry stepped down the hall, he said, "Cheap trick, man," and reached out.

"Phil! Stop!"

169

Too late. As soon as Phil's hand touched the doorknob, his head thrust back and he let out a screaming high pitched yowl. His mouth wrenched open, and the cords of his neck standing out as his eyes bugged out. The scream went on and on as the man stood completely still, frozen in place.

Barry stared down at Phil's hand his eyes wide in shock. Crystals of ice were moving through his fingers, up past his knuckles and to the wrist. Phil was being electrocuted with cold! Barry raised a fist and slashed his arm down with all his might on Phil's wrist, smashing his hand off the knob.

Phil tottered and fell back onto the floor unconscious.

Two of his fingers were still attached to the doorknob.

"Jesus H. Christ!" Barry gasped. He ran to the bathroom and grabbed all the bath towels. He hustled back to Phil and swaddled the man's now thawing and bleeding hand in them. The fingers that had been frozen to the knob had also thawed and were now on the floor. He gathered them up and wrapped them in a towel as well.

Grabbing Phil by the shoulders, he pulled him downstairs and to the backseat of his cab. Slamming his door, he gunned the car and peeled out of the driveway to Kingston General's Emergency Room. Glancing in the rear view mirror, her saw that although Phil was breathing, he was out cold.

The house had been still as he dragged Phil out. Where the hell was Stella? How did Evelyn let this happen?

He and Myra were on their own.

Chapter 20

Myra fished the cell phone from her bag and her eyes flashed wider seeing that it was Barry.

"Hi. How'd it go today?" She turned slightly in her seat, facing the window rather than the teenage boy who had taken the empty spot next to her on the bus.

"Not good. I'm at the hospital."

Her heart leapt to her mouth, "What? Are you okay?" Oh God. She could picture him broken up in a hospital bed with tubes coming out of him everywhere.

"I'm fine. It's Phil. Are you still at work, Myra?"

The fast clip of his words put her senses on high alert. "No. I'm heading home on the bus. What's wrong? What happened to Phil?"

"He hurt his hand. Actually he's probably going to lose it. I don't want you to go in the house alone,

Myra. Whatever was in there is back again. It was stronger today than I've ever seen it."

"What?" The image of Leia's carcass at the house and the upside down tree flashed through her mind. It was supposed to be gone! All the books and websites had said that the cleansing and the priest would do the trick. And Philip? Losing his hand? It couldn't be true.

"Barry what happened?"

He sighed over the phone. "I'm not sure, but my anger at Phil and his grisly escapades in Haiti gave power to whatever's at the house."

"What the hell are you talking about?"

He sighed again. "When he got here, he was pretty skeptical and really sanctimonious... I sorta felt myself rooting for the entity to teach him a lesson..."

"What!"

"Myra, it was just a thought in the back of my mind! And afterwards, when I grabbed him to pull him outta there, I laid the touch on him. Jesus! You have no idea the kind of shit he got into down there in Haiti! He came back home so he couldn't get arrested!"

They were both silent on the phone until Myra said, "So each of you approached the thing with a sullied heart?"

Barry's voice was a whisper. "Yes."

173

"Barry… come home. We'll get this right."

"I can't. I got a lot of questions to answer. The cops are here. I was going to just dump him at the entrance to the Emergency Room, but a nurse saw me. I came up with a story that I found him at the house like this when I got there."

"What the hell is Phil going to say about that?"

"Nothing. He doesn't remember a thing about today."

"Oh." She paused. "I'll meet you at home."

"Are you crazy? Stay on the bus! Go out to the Rose and Crown and I'll meet you there!"

She sat up straighter and her knuckles were ivory gripping the phone. "No Barry. I'm almost there and I'm going home. I'll do the smudge again, light the candles, the holy water, the whole nine yards. It worked last night and by hell it will work again." She jerked down on the bus cord above the window, signaling that she was getting off at the next stop.

"No Myra! Listen to me!"

She clicked the phone off. She got to her feet and waited next to the door, holding the overhead bar until the bus came to a stop. Her knees began to shake, but she ignored the fear.

The entrance to the driveway was across the street. She descended the stairs and stood watching it for a few seconds. She'd had enough of this bullshit. It was bad enough the crap from customers she had to take at work but in her own home? Bullied and scared shitless by a ghost! A ghost! No freakin' way!

Her chin rose high and she squared her shoulders marching across the street to the driveway. The limestone house was deceptively charming, rising from the pristine banks of snow to the gingerbread trim under the gabled roof. From the outside, it could grace the cover of a Currier and Ives Christmas card, a perfect symbol of home and happiness. Yet inside, a malignant cancer had seeped through the very earth it sat on, feeding on fear, growing stronger every day.

Stella had managed it for over sixty years, and together with Evelyn had held the evil forces at bay. Stella had seen that potential in Barry. She'd chosen *him* over a blood relative—her nephew—to carry on the responsibility. If it was just a matter of a haunting, then she and Barry would probably leave. They could get by without the house or the money. But there was more at stake here than just the two of them, if what Stella had written was true.

The headlines in the newspapers were scary enough without the threat of another Hitler or Mussolini being unleashed. The most powerful country in the world, the USA was on the brink of a presidential election. In Europe, the threat of the EU breaking up loomed large. Russia was flexing its muscle in a way

175

reminiscent of the cold war, something it hadn't done in years and years. The world was in a state of flux and this *thing*, this evil entity was doing its best to escape the confines where Stella had kept it.

She shook her head but kept walking up the lane. It seemed crazy that she and Barry, a cab driver and a waitress, could be involved with this, could be instrumental in maintaining order and peace in the world.

But hadn't that been true throughout history? Rosa Parks refusing to go to the back of the bus in the fifties? Her one stand of courage set the wheels in motion for an African American president to be elected! She remembered watching CNN that night and how so many correspondents of color had been thrilled. And Candy Lightener...she'd changed drunk driving laws!

Nope. Individuals can and do make a difference. She didn't ask for this, but she wasn't going to back down. Absently, her hand rubbed her womb as she thought of Isabella.

Well it looked like it was up to them now, doing whatever it took to keep this evil cancer from growing. For a moment her resolve faltered walking by the black car which had to be the priest's. He'd tried and failed. What could she do that would be any better than a priest's blessing?

She climbed the steps and rooted in her purse for the house key, all the while steeling herself once again, for the battle inside. She wasn't going to turn tail and run. Not Myra Sullivan Ryan, thank you very much! Her heart beat hard in her chest and she breathed faster trying not to notice the slight tremor in her fingers fitting the key into the lock.

Too late, she heard the crunch of a heavy boot in the frozen snow behind her. She started to turn but a meaty paw closed over her mouth. Another arm and hand circled her body and gripped her like a vise, lifting her from her feet, thrusting the door wide to totter forward.

"Got you now, bitch!"

Chapter 21

It was what woke him that morning—the voice. It had been right.

'Today we take back the house.'

Gordon had sat straight up in bed, ignoring the rush of bile in the back of his throat from the night of drinking. His head was splitting but that didn't matter. The only thing that was important was the voice and the certainty in his gut that the words were true.

The only other time he'd felt so connected was that time Stella had made him sit in the living room and had grilled him with question after question. He'd just been getting comfortable sitting in the chair by the fire, looking around and feeling good, confident that it would all be his when out of the blue, she'd thrown him out without warning. The voices had been whispering to him that day as well, telling him he belonged there, it was *his* home.

Whatever ability his aunt Stella had...well, he had it too. It was how he'd kept the job at the prison for so many years. He'd known which of the loser inmates he could trust and also the right time to bring dope into work to score some cash. When they did a search, he would help toss the joint, giving such a performance of disgusted outrage that he deserved an Academy Award. They'd never suspected him at all.

The old bitch had known he had the gift too but more than that, her gift was more powerful. She was able to read him, and was repulsed by him.

Everything in his life would change after this night. The house would be his to sell to a developer and the money would be enough that he could retire. Move out of this god forsaken country to someplace warm; some third world country where he'd live like a king. Flash a wad of cash down there and lots of chiquitas would fall all over him. Hot, Latinas who would see him as a rich gringo, not some broken down guy going to pot. Yeah, things were gonna change big time!

After grabbing some rope and the hammer from his tool box, he'd left the townhouse to begin the game of cat and mouse. He'd parked the car just down the street from the driveway and sat waiting and watching. When the black sedan drove into the driveway, he knew in his gut that it was a priest driving it. And the cabbie's taxi wasn't far behind, the stupid cabbie too intent to even notice old Gordo hunched over the steering wheel, watching it all. And what he didn't see, the voice whispered in his head, filling in the details.

Even from a hundred yards away he'd felt the violence and rage in the upstairs bedroom when the priest had entered the house. It was all he could do to stay in the car and not race over to the house to kill them both. But the voice commanded him to stay where he was. When the taxi came hurtling out onto the street, the cabbie's face white as a sheet behind the wheel, he knew he'd been right to listen.

No sooner had the cab disappeared from sight, when he got his next directive. He had gotten out of the car and walked over to the house, hiding in the low laying branches of the evergreen at the side of the house, just the way he'd done that night...How long ago had that been? His mind strained trying to remember it. No matter.

It was like a mirage when the cabbie's wife had come storming down the laneway, her breath pluming in front of her face like some kind of she-dragon, a fire breathing monster. It was comical seeing all five foot nothing of her stomping along the hard packed snow. She was nothing...nothing compared to him in size and smarts. He was going to enjoy crushing her.

He moved quickly and silently, the voice in his head prodding him on. When he grabbed her, raw power surged and pulsed through his body! Even to the point that he got *hard*! That hadn't happened in a long, long time. He'd almost forgotten the thrill of it.

"Got you now, bitch!" He gripped her tight, pressing into her body with his own as they lurched as one into the front hallway.

He looked around, at the archways, the staircase, the high ceilings. It was exactly as he remembered. The trip down memory lane was short lived with the bitch's legs kicking at him, her talons raking the flesh of his hand.

"Fuck!" He threw her to the floor.

She looked up at him with wild blue eyes, her lips pulled back in snarl. The bottom few buttons of the coat had popped open, the dark skirt tangled high on her thighs and her legs scrambled trying to get away from him. For a moment the urge to kick the living shit out of her competed with arousal...to tear her dress higher and—

'NOT HERE! NOT YET!'

His fingers splayed, blood dripping from the rips her nails made in his hand and he jerked back. The roar of the voice filled his head and the whole house. Even the bitch flinched at the sound.

181

She was almost on her feet, screaming, "Get out of my house! Leave me alone or I swear...I swear—"

"Shut up! This is *my* house, not yours! You and your looser husband tricked the old bag!" He stepped closer, batting her back down with his forearm.

The bitch skittered backwards from the blow and she began to fumble for the newel post of the stair. Her eyes narrowed and spittle flew from her mouth when she yelled. *"You're* the nephew?"

His fingers balled into a fist and he struck the side of her face, knocking her head against the carved wooden post. A stream of blood began to flow from her nose and he raised his fist once more.

'STOP!'

His arm froze mid air, unable to move up or down. A jagged pain shot through his head like a buzz saw. He couldn't move a muscle. He could barely breathe! He watched in rage as the woman clutched a spindle of the staircase and hauled herself upright.

'Take her to the cellar.'

The low whisper was a chill that shuddered through his body, breaking the paralyzing spell. He grabbed her foot and yanked her once more to the floor. With his other hand he reefed on her arm, dragging her away from the stairs.

"Let me go!" The woman continued to swat her arm at him and kick her feet.

Her screams would never be heard outside, not with the thickness of the walls and the distance from the street. He needed to hurry though in case the cabbie came home. He wanted her tied up and at his mercy when her husband arrived.

He hauled her down the hallway to the cellar entrance, keeping his arm extended to avoid her thrashing. With his free hand he yanked the door open and tugged her inside. The air was dank and rancid. The bitch retched at the odor, but he inhaled deeply. *It was powerful!* He swelled with the increase of energy that flowed into him. It was the same as the last time when he snuck into the cellar. It was awesome!

The bare light bulb flashed bright when he flipped the switch, lighting the way down the narrow wooden steps. He dragged and clattered down with the woman in tow. Getting to the bottom and feeling the packed earth under his feet elevated the majestic sensation.

There was a metal support post off to the right, which would do for what he had planned.

His head bobbed to the side when the bitch landed a punch above his ear. She was totally wild with strings of hair that escaped her pony tail now framing a heart shaped face twisted with fear, but now, he was

183

MICHELLE DOREY

able to control her with one hand as his power grew. Her eyes were wide and darting everywhere looking for anything to help her.

His fingers closed on the flesh of her cheek, squeezing and twisting until she screamed, her hands tearing at his. Quick as a flash his fingers curled around her pony tail of hair, yanking hard, pulling her forward to the pole. He banged her head against it, smiling at the clanging thud and the flutter of her eyes as she crumpled like a rag doll to the floor.

He took a deep breath and let it out slowly. She was out cold. Tying her hands and feet to the pole would be easy as pie. He took the rope from his overcoat pocket and began with her feet, yanking off her boots and looping the nylon around her ankles.

When he was done that, he hoisted her body up and draped her head and shoulders over his own, repeating the looping around the wrists and then securing the line to the pole. The last was the lines around her waist to keep at least half of her upright.

He stepped back and wiped the sweat that had beaded on his forehead with the back of his hand.

The thud upstairs followed by the cabbie calling 'Myra!' was the icing on the cake. Perfect timing.

<u>Chapter 22</u>

Barry raced out of the emergency room to his cab. He burned rubber, fishtailing down the ramp of the ER parking area onto King Street West.

Why couldn't she have just listened to him? She could be so stubborn sometimes! And this was definitely not the time to be bull headed. God! If she'd seen Philip's hand she wouldn't go near the house on her own!

He hit the button on the steering wheel and spoke, "call Myra." After the connection was made, the ringing just went on and on before voice mail kicked in, setting his nerves even more on edge. Why wasn't she picking up?

He banged the steering wheel with his fist seeing the traffic light turn from amber to red and the car ahead of him slow down to a stop.

Suddenly the scene out the windshield became black and the muscles in his neck became steel cords. Myra was being dragged along the wooden floor by some hulking brute. She kicked and screamed and when the guy's head turned and he snarled at her, Barry's blood turned to ice. It was Gordon! He had Myra! Oh my God, he was taking her down to the cellar!

His vision cleared and the street was once more in front of him. He yanked the steering wheel, whipped past the car in front and ran the light, narrowly missing a pedestrian. He punched the gas.

He was about to hit the button to call her again when the phone rang, startling him.

"Myra?" Another amber light was just ahead and he floored it.

The sound from the phone was a high pitched squeal, like when you dial a fax number by mistake. It stopped and the voice that followed was tinny and far away. "Hurry! He intends to kill her!"

"Who *is* this?" The palms of his hands were sweaty gripping the steering wheel.

"Hurry Barry!" The phone went silent.

It had been a woman's voice, faint as it was. He knew beyond a shadow of a doubt that it had been Evelyn, not Stella.

"Oh God!" He whipped and yanked the car through the streets.

He'd known Gordon was bad news that day he'd caught him in the driveway when they were moving in. Fuck! He'd screwed up, *again*! He could have beaten the thug up...*anything* to keep him away. Myra accused him of being too much of a pacifist, too easy going and now *she* was going to pay the price for him not having the balls to take care of his family!

Up ahead was his driveway and the tail of his car skidded to the side when he wheeled it in. He skidded to a stop, jumped out of the car and froze in shock.

Every branch of every tree was black with crows. Oh God. There were so many, twitching, hunched together, their black eyes peering down at him.

They were absolutely silent and totally malevolent. He reached out to them with the touch and felt them quivering inside like an arrow on a string. All of them were aching to attack him and tear him to pieces before he could take another step. But something—*someone*— was keeping them at bay.

The evil in this house was growing. He knew why—Gordon was here, his treacherous greed feeding it, along with Myra's terror.

Barry sprinted over to the front of the house. Gordon wanted the house, the money...he could have it! He'd do anything to save Myra and the baby!

He stepped inside and froze at the sight before him.

Chapter 23

It was the woman from the bedroom, the one he would swear on a stack of bibles had called him on his cell phone. She stood at the top of the stairs staring down at him, her wide eyes black as coal set in a pale, gaunt face.

Her hand rose and she pointed down the hallway, at the door to the cellar. "Hurry." Her voice sounded like it was coming from a hundred miles away.

He gasped when he noticed the blood spots by the newel post as he ran past. Oh God, please don't let him be too late! "Myra!"

The air was thick and cold on his face when he opened the cellar door. He ignored it and flew down, stopping short at the bottom. Gordon, the small teeth flashing in a sly grin, his eyes narrow with victory sent an icy spike of fear through Barry's gut.

Myra was bent at the waist, her hands behind her back tied to a post. He couldn't see her face, hidden in the hair that hung loose from her pony tail. But the sense that she was still alive was strong. And not just her, but the baby as well.

"Let her go. I'll do anything you want, just don't hurt her." Barry took a few steps down the stairs, holding his hands up, palms out.

"That's close enough." Gordon reached into his coat and pulled out a carpenter's framing hammer. The nail pulling claw stuck out almost straight, like a chisel. He tapped the end of the claw against the side of Myra's head.

Barry threw up his hands in surrender. "Please! Don't!"

Gordon chuckled and lowered the hammer to his side. "I don't want to hurt her. All I want is what's rightfully mine—the house and Stella's estate. Sign it over and I'll let her go." His lips were a snarl when he added, "I don't know how you tricked the old bat, but this was all supposed to go to me."

A trickle of cold sweat dripped down between Barry's shoulder blades. Rather than reassure him, Gordon's words made things worse. The guy was delusional! There was no way he could let either of them live, not after getting the house this way. It wasn't remotely close to being legal and with Barry and Myra alive they could testify to that.

If they had a chance at all, he'd have to play along, buy time until he could overpower him. "Sure. It's yours, Gordon. We'll gladly walk away, just don't hurt her." Barry inched forward another step, still keeping his hands high where Gordon could see them.

Gordon flashed a quick smile and fast as a cat twisted and swung the hammer. The head of the hammer swatted into Myra's tied hands with a sickening thwack.

Barry jerked back and Myra's lurched awake with a scream.

"I told you to stay put!" Gordon once more raised the hammer over Myra's head. "Next time I'll use the claw side!"

Oh shit! This guy was dangerous and fast! Barry's breath was a quick pant, his heart racing hard. "Sorry! What do you want me to do? Do you have the paper? I'll sign!"

Tears streamed from Myra's eyes and her shoulders racked up and down with her keening sobs. Barry's gut knotted with fear.

A sickening grin flared on Gordon's face. "Go upstairs and get a pen and paper. I'll dictate what you need to write." He swung the hammer lightly and struck

Myra's shoulder, making her jerk upright and cry out again. "No funny business, okay? If you try to trick me, the next blow will be in her eye. Got it?"

"No. No, I promise. No tricks. Please, just let us *go*. I'll be right back." Barry spun around and raced up the steps and into the hallway. Once that so-called will was written, Gordon would kill them. There had to be something he could use to distract the man long enough to jump him and get the hammer away.

His gaze flickered over the kitchen table, the counter, washer and dryer as he strode through the room on his way to the library and desk. There was nothing! Nothing that the thug wouldn't spot right away. He had to get Myra away from him!

If Gordon killed them before the will was signed then he'd never get the house. It would go to their estate. He probably knew that.

Barry's eyes narrowed and he grabbed a pen and paper. The will was the only bargaining chip he had and he had to make it count. The chances were slim but better than none at all. As he walked back through the kitchen he noticed the bag of coarse sea salt that Myra had left there when she cleansed the house the day before. Had it just been yesterday?

He slipped the salt into his jacket pocket and was about to step through the doorway to the cellar when movement at the end of the hall caught his eye. It was the woman again. She was floating above the floor slowly coming closer and closer. Her hand rose and she pressed a translucent finger across her lips, signaling for him to stay silent. For just a moment he felt a glimmer of hope that he had an ally that she'd help him beat the monster downstairs holding his wife hostage.

"What are you doing up there?" Gordon's voice was a roar that brought Barry back to the present, but it also served another purpose.

There had been just a hint of anxiety in Gordon's voice. Barry reached out with the touch. Oh no. The gift that Stella had, was present in Gordon as well. It wasn't as strong, but it was still there. He had sensed the ghost that was above him, sensed an enemy. Gordon might have serious allies in the paranormal entities in the house, but he didn't have them all. Whoever this woman was, she was on his and Myra's side.

"Hold on! I'm coming." He spun on his heel and stepped down the few steps to face Gordon. "Before I write anything, I need you to untie my wife."

Gordon raised the hammer again—

Barry had been about to yell for him to stop but Gordon's head jerked back and he slowly lowered the hammer all on his own. His eyes narrowed and head tilted to the side and without another word he stepped to the back of the pole and began untying Myra's hands and then her feet.

A whiff of rotten meat flitted by Barry's face and he recoiled for a moment. The hair on the back of his neck and arms rose and tingled as if an electrical current had passed through his body.

He turned his head and gasped. A pair of red glowing eyes stared over at him from near the furnace. The feeling of rage and malevolence that peered at him made his knees weak.

"There!" Gordon gave Myra a shove. Barry reached for her hand and pulled her close, as much to get her away from Gordon as the thing over by the furnace.

"Start writing! Put your full name and your wife's at the top of the page and write the date." Gordon stepped closer, and Barry knew that with one swing, he could kill Myra. The man was insane!

He took the pen in his hand and started writing on the pad of paper. When he had written what Gordon had ordered he looked up.

"Next line. We relinquish any claim we have on 23 Center Street, and want to adhere to Stella Braithwaite's original wish which was for her nephew Gordon to assume ownership." Gordon stepped closer and his eyes were narrow. "Write it, cabbie!"

A blood curdling scream from Myra filled the room. She had collapsed down onto the floor, rocking back and forth with her arms folded over her belly. Low moans of pain rumbled from her throat.

Oh my God! She was losing the baby! All this pain and horror of Gordon and this...this house. For a second Gordon looked puzzled staring at her. It was now or never!

Barry gripped the pen like a dagger in his hand and lunged at Gordon, passing over Myra and landing on top of the hulking guy. They crashed to the floor, with Barry's fall broken by Gordon's bulk.

He shoved the pen into Gordon's neck, feeling it pierce muscle and tendons. At the same time, he head-butted the man. He was snarling in rage as he pulled at the pen to shove it into Gordon's eye when a force drove down on top of him like a load of bricks.

Every cell in his body exploded in a starburst of agony. The force grasped him in an invisible talon and he was lifted into the air. He couldn't speak nor move! A pain ripped through him, cell by cell.

At the grunt below, he looked down. With horror he saw, Gordon shake his head and grab at the wound in his neck. Damn it, Barry had missed the artery! Gordon rolled to his side and began to struggle to his feet, staring at Myra and licking his lips.

Barry squeezed his eyes tight. FOCUS! He pictured the entity losing power, shrinking back to the floor as it weakened. He felt a shift and his body lowered a little closer to the ground.

In his mind, the energy seeped back into a long fissure in the floor, becoming less and less. He was almost there!

"I command you to release me!" The words rushed out and he felt a jolt when his foot touched the floor.

Gordon spun on his heel, turning to face Barry once more, the hammer raised over his head. With a snarl he rushed at Barry, gibbering with rage.

Barry ducked the blow and pushed forward, his shoulder connecting with Gordon's thigh, flipping the heavy thug over his body. There was a meaty thud, followed by a sharp cry.

Barry pivoted and there was Gordon splayed on the floor, blood pouring from a gash on his head. He took a cautious step forward, his eyes never leaving the hulking inert mass. Gordon wasn't moving. He was either unconscious or dead.

He stepped by Gordon and bent to pick up the hammer but just as his fingers grazed the wooden handle, it whipped away, spinning across the floor and pinging against the stone wall. The stench of rotten meat filled the air and a set of red eyes glared at him.

"Barry, look out!" Myra's voice pierced the air.

Just in time, Barry ducked. The hammer flew through the air, missing his head by a whisker. The evil in the cellar was fighting back. Gordon was down but the danger was far from over.

"Go Myra! Get out of here!" He looked over and saw her gripping the hand rail, trying to get up.

The entity also noticed her. The dark mist began to swirl in her direction.

Salt! Barry's hand thrust into his pocket and closed over the plastic bag of sea salt. He tore it open and filling his fist he threw a handful at the thing. "Leave!"

The thing stopped and shrank back, turning to face him. But there was no way that he was going to stop now, especially seeing Myra scramble up the next step, getting away from the danger. He kept advancing until his fingers invaded the revolting mass, becoming numb as soon as he grasped the gelatinous mass.

Eyes formed and flared and for a moment Barry saw more detail of the thing's face, the gaunt hollow under the cheekbones, its ears and bare head. Oh God! There were fucking ram's horns sprouting from its forehead...a split tongue shot out from a gaping mouth. What the hell was he dealing with?

"LEGION!" The voice roared in a chorus of hundreds!

The roar sent new shock waves through Barry's chest. The beast in his hands gave a lurch and flew off, crashing into the furnace. The ley line was ripping apart!

Dirt and objects began to fly through the air, blinding him. The furnace door burst open and a flash of fire shot out, singing his leg. He lurched to the side, his hand pounding at the smoldering fabric covering his thigh.

"Barry!" Myra's voice sounded a million miles away in the turmoil of flying objects, the voices and whispers filling the air around him.

"Go! Get out Myra! Run!" He couldn't see her because the beast was coming at him, now a cloud of black mist again, roiling over him, making him numb. And, oh so cold as it crept up his legs to his chest. He couldn't move. The salt in his fist slipped out over his chest as the feeling left his fingers. The numbing cold crept higher up his body. Soon he wouldn't be able to speak or breathe.

He felt helpless as a child in the face of this evil. He'd done all that he could and it hadn't been enough. The most he could pray was that Myra would get away, that she and the baby would be safe. A knot of ice crept into his chest and he lurched back, trying to escape searing, jagged cold.

He hadn't been prepared for this. Hadn't known how bad, bad could be. "Oh God, please help me."

An inhuman laugh filled the room. "He won't help you, you fool!"

The air became thick and hard to breathe...

"Barry!" Myra's voice was the last thing he heard as he drifted into unconsciousness.

Chapter 24

Tears burned Myra's eyes when she stood at the top step looking down into the cellar. She could hardly make out Barry on the floor with the smoke and whirling debris. The pain in her smashed hand was nothing to the horror in her chest watching her husband, overcome by the evil below.

"Barry!" She took a step lower. She had to try! She couldn't just leave him there!

Behind her the door to the cellar burst open with a thundering crash. She spun around. A woman stood there, dark hair framing a face that was filled with anger. Her eyes were round and black as coal when she came through the doorway. Her clothes were from another time period, a long dress and lace falling from her sleeves.

Myra could only stare in shock at the wispy apparition before her. This was no woman—she was floating above the floor!

"Go. Protect the baby." The words drifted in the air but the woman's mouth hadn't moved.

As if. She turned to look down the stairs at Barry's writhing body. "That's my *husband*!"

The apparition lifted a finger. "What happens here will end here, Myra. Your child is our hope."

Another moaning cry from Barry came up the stairs. Looking down she could barely discern his form under the rippling purple mist covering him.

A jab of pain pierced her hand when she put it against the wall to support her. An idea sparked in her mind and she reached out to the figure before her.

"Please help him!" she gasped, but her hand passed through the specter. How in the world could something so ephemeral be any help?

The woman and the ghost passed through one another and Myra ran to the foyer where Reverend Phil had left his valise. She had tripped over it when Gordon dragged her into the house. She hunkered down to the floor and rummaged in it with her good hand. She pulled out a small gold bottle, not much bigger than a salt shaker. Engraved on the side was 'Sacred Chrism'. Whatever blessing the priest had tried hadn't worked.

Neither Father Phil nor Barry had pure hearts when they tried. But when she performed *her* ritual the other night things had quieted down.

"Shit!" It was capped and there was no way she'd ever get the bottle open. But there was no time to lose. Barry needed her. She raced back to the cellar.

The spectral woman was at the bottom of the stairs. She was floating above Barry's prostrate figure and had her arms outstretched like she was trying to hold something back.

Wrapped in swirling billows of red, purple and black, the entity that crawled out from the bowels of the earth was poised like a hyena about to strike. Myra could see its red eyes glitter brightly, and as she came down the steps, the swirls would part for a second revealing an oozing maw.

It grinned as it drew closer to the woman and Barry.

The air was filled with a cacophony of wind and clanging metallic bangs as the two apparitions confronted each other.

Evelyn, despite her efforts, was being overwhelmed. She was being pushed away from Barry and her image was becoming foggier and foggier.

Halfway down the stairs, Myra held the bottle high and called out in a quivering voice "In the name of God, I command you to leave!"

She held her breath. Her hand holding the bottle of Chrism was shaking as much as her legs when the being looked away from Evelyn to her. Its eyes sparked even brighter and its maw yawned open like a hyena about to strike and she recoiled, arching her back.

In that instant Stella's words echoed in her head. *The thing feeds on fear. Fear not. Be not afraid!*

She closed her eyes and spoke aloud. "Yea, though I walk in the valley of death…" opening her eyes, she continued, "I SHALL FEAR NO EVIL!" Holding onto the thinnest reed of faith in the goodness of the universe, she took a deep breath. "In the name of God and all that is *love*, in the name of God and all that is *life*, in the name of God and all that is *joy* get thee hence from here!"

Tears stung her eyes as the power of her faith consumed her. She descended each step, waving the golden bottle before her as a talisman of hope.

"The will of love commands you! Be gone!" She stepped again.

"The will of hope commands you! Leave this realm!" Again, she stepped down.

The being had stopped its advance. Its eyes grew huge, but now the glee that had been in them was a mortal rage. The room thundered with its hate and buffeted her like a unstoppable wave.

"The will of God commands you!" She held herself upright as best she could, and felt Isabella kick in her womb.

So be it. She stepped over to Barry's form. They'd stand or fall as a family. With an agony she didn't know could exist firing though her broken hand, she pulled the stopper from the bottle of Chrism and threw it at the beast. It passed through the figure like a bullet.

The demon recoiled.

Now raising the open bottle she shook its neck at the beast, splashing it with the blessed oil and balsam mixture.

Over and over she screamed every word she knew of goodness as she lashed at and advanced on this terrible visage, emptying the container.

"Light!"

"Love!"

"Joy!"

"Barry!"

"Isabella!"

"Mother!"

"Father!"

"To life!"

With each cry her faith grew.

And the savage shrank back. It folded into itself, collapsing smaller and smaller.

The Evelyn apparition now pressed the advantage floating closer and closer. Her fingers were curved talons reaching for the thing. It passed Myra and engaged the beast directly. As the beast waned, the woman waxed, forcing it lower and lower.

Throwing the now empty bottle at the two figures, Myra turned to Barry's still form. She dropped to her knees onto the dirt floor and clutched his head. "Barry!" She couldn't even tell if he was breathing! Again and again she called his name. "Please come back! I love you!" Tears flowed down her face and dripped onto her husband's. She leaned in and kissed his forehead, his cheeks, his lips, crying and keening all the while, like an animal caught in a leg trap.

He was so cold. What a horrible price they were paying to be good.

It wasn't supposed to be like this! Her hands curled into fists and she beat his chest. "Wake up!" In the dream she had a lifetime ago, he died because she

205

had not been there when he needed her. But that hadn't happened!

She pounded and pushed his chest over his heart over and over. She stopped for a moment, watching for any response. Nothing. Her chin dropped to her chest and her shoulders wracked as more tears fell through her now closed eyes.

Like a warm blanket the presence of the woman spirit enveloped her and Barry. The energy tingled warm through her body. Opening her eyes she saw Evelyn's face before her. She dropped her head to see the woman's now almost solid hand rest on Barry's heart. At the same time, her daughter moved again deep inside.

A pure white glow of energy now flowed through both her and Barry in a swirling cascade of warmth and joy. A sense of peace filled her.

She stroked her husband's still face. With a sad smile, she said, "Thy will be done," over and over. They had fought the good fight for a greater good.

"Thy will be done."

She jerked back when Barry sat bolt upright. A loud sucking sound followed as he gasped a lungful of air. "OOoooHHHhhEEEE" he screamed as he struggled to breathe. Over and over again he hooted and hacked rattling coughs trying to catch his breath.

"Barry!" She pulled him in and hugged him like she'd never let go.

He coughed a couple of times and pulled back, straining to get to his feet. "Where—"

"It's gone." She looked around. Evelyn had also vanished. She clutched him again. "I thought you were dead!"

Barry held onto to her and they rocked together. "I... I think I was," he said in a voice filled with awe. He gazed around the cellar. When he saw the still form of Gordon his head jerked back. "He's dead." It wasn't a question, just a statement of fact.

His face showed concern and he leaned closer putting his hand on the back of her head. "Myra. He hurt you. We've got to get you to the hospital." He lowered his hand to her waist and stroked softly and sighed, "Thank God, the baby's fine."

The pain flared through her hand like a flame. She dropped her head. Bones would knit and life would go on. They were together, a family. They had faced and fought absolute evil and beat it back empowered by love and hope. That was the force that was stronger than what had invaded the house.

She looked over at Gordon and for a moment she felt sorry for him. He had let himself be such an easy prey. The evil in the house had used and discarded him like a paper towel.

207

"We've got to call the police before I can go to get fixed up. How the hell are we ever going to explain what happened?" She reached for his hand and together the two of them helped each other get to their feet. After all that had happened both of them were drained.

"We're not. Leave it to me."

Chapter 25

Barry and his Dad stood at the kitchen sink washing the last of the pots and pans from the Christmas feast. Even though he'd prepared the meal and got everything ready for the big dinner, Barry was content to finish the day working next to his father. Holiday family gatherings were always bitter sweet without his Mom being there.

Besides which, with Myra's busted hand she was better off sitting in the living room with Tony and his family. The sounds of laughter and good natured protests whenever someone scored a point in the board game they were playing drifted into the kitchen, making him smile. The fact that the whole atmosphere of that room had changed so much that it was actually pleasant to sit there, also made him smile.

"Myra is lucky to be alive." His Dad finished drying the pot and set it on the counter. He looked over at Barry and shook his head. "I'm sorry, but I just can't get over that guy attacking her."

"Yeah. He must have had a few screws loose to begin with but when Stella left the house to me, he totally lost it. He actually thought that he'd get the house if I signed some paper."

"Crazy." His father's eyebrows drew together. "Thank God you came home when you did." He paused and his eyes were intense watching Barry. "But I've got a feeling there's more to it than what you told the police, right?"

Barry sighed and looked over his shoulder towards the doorway. Myra's family were still laughing and playing the board game. It was just the two of them there and high time for honest talk. "Yeah, quite a bit more. The house is—"

"Haunted." His father let out a short laugh and tilted his head looking towards the ceiling. "I knew it the first day I stepped inside here." He tossed the tea towel over his shoulder and wandered over to the kitchen table. "This was the Stella's favorite spot to sit in this house. I saw her here the day we helped you move in."

Barry turned and did a double take before shaking his head. "Dad! You saw her? You have *the touch*?"

210

"Where do you think you got it?" He sat back and laced his hands at the back of his head, looking over at his son.

Barry let the water out of the sink and dried his hands before joining his father at the table. "Did Mom know? She never said anything to me about it."

"I only have it to a slight degree Barry...nothing like what *you* have. So, no she never knew. She was always so proud of you and your gift. I didn't see any need to mention where you got it from." His dark eyes became soft with sadness and he looked down at the table, lost in some memory for a few moments.

Barry sat silent for a few moments debating whether to bring this up. They'd each been lost in grief after his mother had been killed and had never talked much about that day.

"Dad? I've always felt guilty about her death."

"Yeah, I know. I tried to talk to you about it, but you kept pushing me away."

He couldn't bring himself to look his father in the eye. "I could have saved her, Dad."

"Because of your premonition?"

Barry looked up sharply, in stunned silence.

Dad nodded. "*That* much I was able to sense." He reached out and put his hand on Barry's shoulder. "I know you had one. So did I."

211

"Why didn't you stop her that day?"

"I tried!" I made her promise to not leave the house that day. *She promised*!" Dad shook his head slowly. "We'll never know what caused her to go out in the car that day, Barry, and it doesn't matter. She made her choice."

"But if I said something, that would have been enough!"

"No, Barry, it wouldn't."

"How the hell do you know?"

Dad held his hands out palms up. "Because *she* knew it was a dangerous day too." He ran his hands through his hair. "I've tried for more than twenty years to get through to you about this, buddy." He leaned across the table to his son. "She had a premonition dream the night before. She woke up, and woke me up about it." He shrugged. "That's when I told her that I had a bad feeling and she made the promise not to leave the house." He sighed and looked away. "A promise she broke... not just to me, but to herself."

"But WHY?"

"I don't know! But that's what happened!" Dad sat back in his chair. "Look, if you want to...be my guest and keep blaming yourself. But that's a road that goes nowhere, Barry. You also were just a boy; cut that kid some slack for God's sake!"

Barry sat in silence, sharing the space and time with his father. "I'm going to have to chew this over, Dad."

"Sure. Take all the time you need."

Even so, he felt a weight lift from his heart. "I don't think it'll take long."

Chapter 26

Three years later...

The whole family was outside in the back yard, decked out with party hats, eating hot dogs and potato salad for Isabella's third birthday. Barry didn't bother going inside after parking his cab in the driveway. He just followed the sounds of laughter and the shrieks of joy from Isabella who was playing with her older cousins.

He walked over to Myra and planted a kiss on her forehead. "Sorry I'm late. I got flagged for a fare to go to the train station. Did I miss anything?"

Her smile was mysterious like the Mona Lisa and she took his hand and placed it on her beach ball belly. "Just your son doing cartwheels inside here." She looked over at her daughter and smiled. "Izzy's having a ball."

It was at that moment that his daughter turned her round chocolate colored eyes up and saw him. "Daddy!" She was a bouncing whirlwind of dark curls, a twirling purple skirt and outstretched arms running over to him.

His heart floated high in his chest seeing his daughter. "Isabella! Happy birthday!"

Her arms circled his neck when he picked her up and spun her around in a circle. "You got it for me! I know you did!"

"What? You don't know that! Maybe I got you something else. Something you'll like more." He looked into her eyes but it was hard to keep the grin from his face, teasing her. Of course he'd got her what she asked for. The kitten was in a carrier on the front step.

"I'm going to call her Princess. Where is she?" She squirmed and pushed at his shoulders trying to get back down on the ground.

He took her hand and together they walked around to the front of the house. The pure white kitten extended an arm out one of the holes of the cage trying to play with a leaf.

"Holy doodle! She's so cute!" Isabella raced over to the cage.

Barry stopped in his tracks and watched her. Holy doodle? He had never used that phrase around her and for sure Myra wouldn't. The only other person who he'd ever heard say 'holy doodle' was...

Stella.

His mouth fell open as he watched her open the cage and scoop the kitten out.

He'd never rejected the idea of reincarnation or any other alternative eastern mythology or religion. No one had the absolute goods on anything after this life here on earth. The last time he'd spoken to Stella she had said that energy never dies, it just changes.

Changes into what?

Or into who?

He shook his head with a small smile. Izzy is Izzy.

Isn't she?

Whatever.

Myra came around the corner of the house and reached for his hand, joining him. "I can see why the kitten is her favourite present." She looked up at him. "It reminds me of Leia."

"That's why I picked a white one. It's a female so...who knows? It might have kittens. She's going to call it Princess."

At the sound of a 'caw' high in the apple tree he looked up into its branches. Sitting on the highest limb was a lone crow returning his gaze. He huffed.

There wasn't a day that went by that that harbinger of evil didn't make its presence known at some point. Barry's eyes narrowed for a moment watching it. He'd come to terms with his 'gift' and the power that was within him to safeguard the house and the ley line it sat on. It was as much a part of him and his life as eating or sleeping. There were times that he felt the energy of the magnetic lines flowing into him, increasing his awareness of all that was good in the world—his wife and family.

Suddenly the bird let out a surprised shrill screech and slipped off the branch, flapping its wings wildly. It recovered quickly from its tumble, and lit out across the driveway, over the hedges and out of sight. Its outraged screeches and cackles faded.

"What the—" Barry wondered. He hadn't done anything to drive it away. He turned and saw Isabella on her feet, holding the kitten tight to her body and staring up to where the bird had disappeared.

Isabella walked over to stand in front of her parents and smiled up at them. "Horrible bird. I took care of it this time, Daddy."

The End

A Note From The Author

This tale of The Hauntings of Kingston was inspired by a particular building in my city—it's known as Roselawn House. It was built by a lawyer for his growing family in 1841. Today it still stands; and many of the trees that were planted when it was built survive. It's a beautiful building that has called to me since I was a child. The tale you've just read is of my own imagination that I spun out on the grounds of Roselawn House by asking myself the two word question that so often begins the spinning of a tale:

"What if…"

Thank you for reading this book. Hopefully, you enjoyed it. If you did, please leave a review on Amazon. Reviews help struggling authors get their books in front of more readers. If for any reason, this book missed the mark for you, please accept my apologies. Hundreds of hours went into its creation and all I can say is "I did my best." If you want to let me know where it fell short, there will be no bad feelings on my part, I promise. I will take your feedback to heart, and try to improve—if not on this one, then certainly on the next.

MICHELLE DOREY

Other Tales of
The Hauntings Of Kingston

Crawley House

The Haunted Inn

MICHELLE DOREY